WORLDWAKER

BOOKS BY DEAN F. WILSON

THE CHILDREN OF TELM

Book One: The Call of Agon
Book Two: The Road to Rebirth
Book Three: The Chains of War

THE GREAT IRON WAR

Hopebreaker
Lifemaker
Skyshaker
Landquaker
Worldwaker
Hometaker

THE GREAT IRON WAR - BOOK FIVE

WORLDWAKER

DEAN F. WILSON

Cover illustration by Duy Phan

First Edition 2016

ISBN 978-1-909356-15-3

Published by Dioscuri Press
Dublin, Ireland

www.dioscuripress.com
enquiries@dioscuripress.com

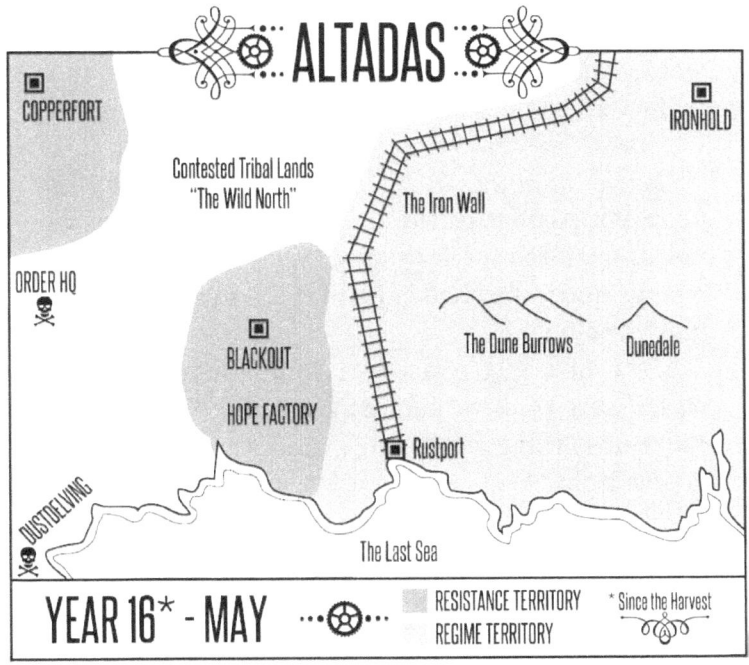

ALTADAS

COPPERFORT

IRONHOLD

Contested Tribal Lands
"The Wild North"

The Iron Wall

ORDER HQ

BLACKOUT

The Dune Burrows

Dunedale

HOPE FACTORY

Rustport

DUSTDELVING

The Last Sea

YEAR 16* - MAY

RESISTANCE TERRITORY
REGIME TERRITORY

* Since the Harvest

THE GREAT IRON WAR

In the world of Altadas, in the year 1888 of the Second Era, women everywhere dreamed of a coming desert. Those who were already pregnant miscarried, and those who became pregnant did not give birth to human children. An invasion had begun.

The newborns had no horns or marks, and so they were loved and reared like all the others. It would take time before anyone realised what they really were, before anyone would call them demons.

These events were marked by the arrival of strangers claiming to be from a distant land. The people of Altadas called them Pilgrims, but they did not know just how far they had come, nor by what strange doors they had entered, nor exactly what they had come for.

The first Pilgrims were scouts, but subsequent waves were soldiers, sent by a man who would later call himself the Iron Emperor. He promised his people iron. He gave them war instead.

They called that year the Harvest, and it became the first year of a new, darker calendar. Sand swept through the great chasms in the sky from where the demons came, the dust of a world that they had dried up. Ahead of the landships went great sandstorms, until the green grasses became an endless red desert.

In Altadas, steam powers industry, but iron powers war. The abundant metal, idolised by the invaders, and depleted in their home world, became a beacon to the demons, and was the foundation upon which they would build their new civilisation. They called themselves the Iron Empire. Their enemies simply called them the Regime.

As war began in the east, few among the Resistance knew that their own children were not really theirs. The invaders had mastered a magical technique to control the birth channels of a people they desired to conquer. Thus with one hand they would wield might, and with the other they would use guile, infiltrating and eradicating their enemies, anyone who would dare defy the Iron Emperor, who had brought his people to this promised land.

Yet iron is more to the demons than just a metal. When broken down into its basic elements, it provides the key ingredient of the necessary sustenance of the invaders. To some it is a drug. To them, symbolising everything they were promised, and everything they were leaving behind, it is Hope.

As one civilisation crumbled, and a new empire was founded on its remains, there were some who refused to live out their last days under the iron grip of their new ruler. They made a promise of their own: to fight, with everything they had, for the fate of humanity.

Thus began the Great Iron War.

CONTENTS

Chapter

Chapter One

PIECES

The panic that swept the sands was like that first experienced by the people of Altadas when the Rift opened in the east, out of which came an invading force like no other. Now, they did not fear any compass direction. The onslaught came from above. The invasion was in their minds.

"We have to shoot it down," Leadman ordered. His men brought their own scopes, none as powerful as Brooklyn's creation, but they were enough to see the little dot in the heavens that made everyone on earth quiver, and enough to aim their sniper rifles.

"No!" Rommond cried as one of the soldiers fired into the air. It was a token shot, a paltry warning to the wind. Whatever message it carried would never reach the hull of the aeroplane, nor the ears of its psychotic crew. Yet Rommond still snatched the gun from the soldier's hands, casting it far away into the dunes.

Leadman's gargantuan jaw dropped at Rommond's display. "You've got some nerve—"

"Are you crazy?" the general interjected. Jacob wondered if the question was perhaps rhetorical.

"We've got to do something, Rommond," Leadman replied.

"That *thing* up there can destroy us all!" Rommond barked, waving an angry finger to the clouds. "You won't just take the sky with it. You'll take the land as well."

"Maybe you should have thought about that before you started looking at unorthodox ways to end this war," the opposing general said. "At least I'm sticking to good old-fashioned guns. *You* created this mess. I'm just trying to clean it up."

Rommond tried to mouth a reply, but the words were crushed by the frustration in his face, leaving just the splinters of sounds mixed with an embittered sigh. He held his hand up, palm outwards, and shook his head, before turning away and limping off to the nearby steamtruck.

"Get out," he told the driver. Few had to be told that twice by Rommond. That list grew fewer all the time. This driver was not one of them. He scrambled out, as if Rommond was the bomb.

The general clambered inside, gritting his teeth as his injuries ganged up to remind him of their presence. All he wanted was to be alone, but the loneliness let him feel the pain even more. He felt the mix of dry and wet blood upon his back, the bruises on his limbs, the thumping headache in his brain. If only those were all of his problems.

The image of the Worldwaker swam in his mind, the shark emblazoned on the bomb taunting him from his memory. That was his idea, an off-the-cuff remark to Doctor Elbern, the head of research at the top-secret Project Ironending. He could feel the Great

Iron War coming to an end now, but he no longer had his finger on the button. The curtains of the world were about to close, and the play of life would soon be over. There would be no applause.

He tried to think of what to do, but he felt helpless. He was always the man with the plan, the great strategist that current historians—who were few and far between, and all in hiding—were writing about. He had no big plan for this. He had not prepared for the day when he would be fighting his own work. He had not plotted against his own plots.

The frustration grew too much. He let it out by thumping the dashboard with his fist. It helped a little, but then he hoped the soldiers outside could not see his moment of weakness. From the corner of his eye, he could see Taberah rounding them up, drawing their attention away from him. She too knew what was at stake. He did not need them waking up to the realisation that their leader in this war was merely human, that he could be broken like the rest of them.

The door on the other side creaked open, and Brooklyn climbed in. He closed the door and sat there in silence for a moment. "Odd," he said in time.

"What's odd?" Rommond asked, his voice much weaker than normal, his tone infused with resignation.

"Odd you think you can hide here," Brooklyn replied.

"I'm tired," Rommond said. "I'm tired of it all. Of war. Of fighting. I don't feel like we're getting anywhere. Each success becomes another failure."

"So you want to sleep, and Armageddon Brigade want to wake you."

Rommond sighed.

"Too bad," Brooklyn said. "Leaders don't get to sleep. This seat is no bed. It is driving seat. You drive. You lead. This truck is no bunker. And that," he said, pointing upwards, "is what you call, I think, bunker-buster."

"If the bunker was the world."

"But it is not world," the tribesman said, placing his hand on Rommond's. "We have no bunker from our troubles. We cannot hide from them. We must face them out in open, under sky." He paused and looked deeply into the general's forlorn eyes. "*In* sky."

"They'll never fly," Rommond said, as Brooklyn conjured the image of his aeroplane designs into his mind. It was a special kind of magic to be able to communicate without words.

"There is many tonnes of wood and metal up there that fly."

Rommond shrugged. "I suppose it's worth a shot."

"Ricochet Rommond," Brooklyn said, "only needs single shot."

When Rommond emerged, Leadman was already making plans, leaning over a giant cloth map stretched over the sand and held down by several tyres. The opposing general continued to issue commands even when he became aware of Rommond's presence.

"From what we can see," Leadman said, pointing his spyglass to the map, "the target is circling the area, but making slow gestures towards an easterly direction." He drew the spyglass across the map, pointing towards the north-east corner. "It seems likely it is heading, however slowly, towards Ironhold."

"Do continue," Rommond said.

Leadman ground his teeth, keenly aware that some of the soldiers were eager to roll up the map and fall into line now that the real commander had arrived.

"If Ironhold is our target's target—"

"If," Rommond interjected, stressing the word, like the hiss of a fuse.

"—then all we have to do is … sit back and wait."

Rommond rolled his eyes. "Isn't that what you've been doing most of this war in Copperfort? Sitting back and waiting for someone else to win this war for you?"

Leadman snapped his spyglass shut. "Why should we do anything to stop this bomb if it is meant for the Iron Emperor's home?"

"Because it will destroy far more than just Ironhold. Because even Ironhold has many innocent people."

"Are you worried that it will get into the wrong hands?"

"It's already in the wrong hands!"

"Then what do we do, Rommond? We can't do nothing and we can't shoot it out of the skies. Where does that leave us?"

"We have to capture it."

Leadman laughed. "You're serious?" he asked, when met with Rommond's glower.

"When have I never been?"

"Well," Leadman said, "we all thought you might have finally *cracked*."

Rommond responded with a glare.

"The question is," Jacob said, "why is it circling here? Why is it not heading straight to Ironhold?"

"I wonder that too," Rommond replied.

"Maybe they *want* us to follow them," Leadman said. "Maybe they're trying to get rid of both us and the Regime in one fell swoop. Round us up and bombs away!"

"Maybe that's their mission," Rommond said, "but this is ours. We need to get into the sky and take back the Worldwaker."

"Like we took back the Landquaker?" Leadman reminded him.

Rommond chewed his lip. "We got it back."

"Not in one piece. And if you don't get that bomb back in one piece, where does that leave us, huh?"

"It leaves us everywhere," the general said, "in little pieces of our own."

Chapter Two

A FOREIGN IDEA

Rommond pulled Taberah aside, as he often did when he was unsure of the road ahead. They were often at odds with one another on how to proceed, which was what made her valuable. Too many of his men were frightened to ever question him. It was the gift and curse of loyalty and discipline.

"Tabs, I need you to—"

"I can't," she interrupted. "I can't go with you."

Rommond could not utter his disbelief.

"I have my own mission," she explained. "She gave it to me."

"Your own mission? Who gave it to you?"

"You wouldn't understand, but I have to do this."

"You're turning your back on this war now? After everything?"

"No," she said. "I'm finally waking up to where my battle is. There's another front, Rommond, and we've got no one fighting there. We could win it all here, but it will be for nothing if we can't win there too."

Rommond smacked the palm of his hand to his face. "God, Tabs. If that thing goes off up there, or down here, or any bloody place else, there won't be any more war! There won't be any more *anything*! It'll all be over. This front. That front. None of it will matter! Right now *this* is our priority." He reached his hand out, pleading with her. "Can't you see that, Tabs? Can't you see?"

"It isn't my priority," Taberah replied. "I'm sorry, but that's the truth. I know you don't get it, Rommond, but I can't ignore this. I've let this part of me sleep too long. The more I've tip-toed around it, the more it feels like I'm treading glass. Some day the pain will get too much, and I'll scream. And it'll wake up. I have to wake it gently now."

"Don't abandon us, Tabs," Rommond said. "I gave you everything I could to keep you on board, to keep you on our side. You feel like you're treading glass now? I've been doing that my whole life, trying to keep the troops in order, trying to stop the Resistance from splintering apart. How many of us were there in the early days? And I don't just mean those who died. Some left willingly. One of those was you. Don't leave again."

He was ashamed to see pity in her eyes, but thankful that she tried to hide it.

"You helped me find my path back then," she said. "The Glassfinder Project gave me purpose. With the amulets, I could stop others from experiencing what I experienced. I'm just finishing what I started."

"You'll never be finished that. You can't chase ghosts forever in this world."

She gave a resigned smile, as if he had read the final page from the journal of her mind.

"No," Rommond said, shaking his head violently.

He pointed aggressively at her, and his hand shook to match his voice. "You keep fighting. You keep fighting *here*. You have people here you need to fight for."

"I know," she whispered, but it sounded like she was already leaving.

When the general consoled in Brooklyn, he was shocked to find the tribesman was heading off on his own mission too. Rommond never expected him to fly one of the planes, just like he generally avoided driving landships, but he hated the idea of Brooklyn willingly going back into Regime territory.

"Why can't you just sit this one out?" the general asked him. "We need people in Blackout too."

"But really you need me to be old self," Brooklyn said. "Much of me is back there with Controller."

"What if she wants you to go back? What if she's controlling you now?"

"Either way, I have to go. I have to find out. I have to find me."

"What if you don't come back?"

The thought was horrifying. Rommond was not sure he could withstand losing Brooklyn again. Though he was not the same as he was before, it was still him, or a part of him. It was something. He dared not think of how he would cope if Brooklyn did not return.

Brooklyn held the general's hand between both of his. "But what if I do?"

As time ticked dangerously away, Rommond summoned anyone and everyone who might have even had the potential of a plan. They decided not to return to Blackout, in case the word got out, and panic undid the order that Rommond had worked so hard to establish there.

"We need to get airborne," the general said.

"Pity we wasted the Skyshaker," Cantro replied.

"It wasn't wasted."

"So, I presume you checked out those Regime schematics for Brooklyn's aeroplanes?" Jacob asked. "Seems they were useful after all."

"We did, and they all carry the emblem of a military base attached to the coastal town of Rustport, at the very southern tip of the now toppled Iron Wall."

"Pity we wasted the Landquaker," Leadman jeered.

With Rommond, you did not ruffle his feathers— you ruffled his moustache. Right then, his moustache shuddered. "Well, the spyglass to the past is a lot clearer than the one to the future."

"You're telling me," Jacob said.

"So, how do you propose we take Rustport?" Leadman wondered.

Rommond sighed. "I don't know how we're going to do it. We've lost too many people, and too many vehicles. There's little hope of us storming Rustport. And yet … we have to try."

"Well, assaulting the Iron Wall didn't look too likely to succeed," Jacob reminded them, "and here we are."

"But why do we have to try?" Whistler asked.

Everyone turned to him, bemused. Though there were people his age fighting on the Regime side, most of those present still saw him as a child, despite the growing crackle in his voice. The wind played with his curls, which were so at odds with all the skin-tight haircuts of the soldiers present.

"I mean … why do we have to fight?" he explained, though that did little to help their confusion.

"I don't follow," the general said. War was not so much a career for him as it was his entire life. Jacob wondered if he was born in uniform. The smuggler knew what Whistler was getting at, but he also understood why Rommond did not.

Some were already turning back to the battle map.

"Let's hear him out," Jacob said. "He's been helpful before." He gave the boy a reassuring nudge of his elbow.

"Go on then," Rommond said.

"Well, uh … why can't we just, you know, team up?"

The expression on Rommond's face showed that he still did not quite follow. The idea was so foreign to him that it might as well have been in another language—maybe even a demonic one.

"Team up?" the general asked, stressing the words, as if he was desperately trying to comprehend. It was a simple idea, too simple for the plotters and schemers of war.

Whistler folded his arms, revealing the coloured patches on his elbows. "Why not? They don't want to get killed by the bomb. And, uh, we don't either. So, instead of us fighting them, and them fighting us … why not fight on the same side?"

There was a round of laughter from many of the tacticians standing there. More turned back to the map, assuming Whistler was drafted in as a bit of entertainment. Gregan, Leadman's right-hand man, was particularly vocal in his snickers.

Jacob could tell that Whistler was growing frustrated that people were treating his idea like a joke, so he thought it best he intervened. He felt like he was intervening a lot lately. *So much for this not being my war*.

"Is it that strange an idea?" he asked them. Because he was an adult, they paid him more heed. "I mean, stranger things have happened before. So we've been enemies all this time, but now there's a bigger threat. It's bigger than all of us. It's bigger than sides, bigger than war."

"Ridiculous!" Gregan cried. "They're our *enemy*!"

"Even if we agreed to it," Cantro said, "there's no chance they'd do the same."

"Why isn't there?" Whistler asked. "Have you tried?"

"He make good point," Brooklyn said. "Did we not think tribes would not join us? How can we win if we defeat ourselves in mind before battle?"

"Watch Rommond break," Gregan whispered to Leadman, though not quiet enough that others could not hear. "One word from Oobi-ooba-luga, or whatever he's called, and Rommond's will crumbles." Leadman gave the slightest of smiles, accentuated by his massive jaw.

Whistler looked up at Jacob with worried eyes. They were both glad that Rommond was too preoccupied to overhear.

"This is against my better judgement," the general said, "but I've been wrong in the past, and my better judgement hasn't yet ended this war. I've been fighting for so long now that I've almost forgotten what it's like to make peace." He paused and bit his lip, before shaking his head. "Nothing makes this feel right to me, but at this moment there is a bigger threat out there, a mutual enemy. Maybe the war will begin anew when we defeat it, but if we can secure a momentary truce, then that is all we need ... for now."

"Madness!" Gregan roared. "I can't believe you're all just standing there, letting this idiocy happen. If we lay down our guns to these ... these *monsters* ... then you can bet they'll pick them up and use them against us. You're proposing we surrender!"

"We're not doing anything of the sort," Rommond responded.

"You're all cowards," Gregan said, aiming his index finger at the crowd. "A moment ago you're rooting for war, and with one word from Rommond you're braying for peace. And I *know* how you feel about those demons. Why won't you say anything?"

"That's enough now," Leadman said, grabbing him by the arm.

Gregan humphed, ripping his arm from Leadman's grasp. "I'd have thought you, of all people, would have had more of a bite!"

Leadman grabbed Gregan by the collar and dragged him away from the crowd, out of earshot, but not out of sight. They watched awkwardly as the ageing general showed the younger lieutenant that he still had plenty of bite.

Rommond looked at Brooklyn, who shrugged his eyebrows, but kept his mouth firmly shut.

"Well," Jacob said, "nothing like us turning on ourselves to start off the truce."

Chapter Three

VOLUNTEERS

A series of makeshift tents were erected halfway between Blackout and the Iron Wall. Word got back to the Baroness Ebronah about the bomb, and she swiftly sent supplies to bolster the ragtag band of people plotting a solution in the desert.

Rommond laid out the Regime schematics of Brooklyn's aeroplane designs. There were several variations, and the stamped dates showed a progression of improvements to the aerodynamics and stability. There were older, more rugged biplanes, with the two sets of wings on the top and bottom attached together with poles. There were also the lighter, faster monoplanes, with just one set of wings, and these were the ones that the general was most interested in.

"The Long Spyglass shows that the plane the Armageddon Brigade is using, rather appropriately dubbed the Dreamdevil, is an older, more cumbersome design," he explained. "Maybe they have others, but the weight of the bomb required they use the most stable option, which is a much larger, and thankfully much slower, biplane. These monoplanes are considerably faster, and might just afford us enough time to catch up with it before they reach Ironhold."

"How do we know the Regime has even made these?" Jacob asked.

Rommond prodded the documents. "The papers are marked with the inventory, and dated. They had eighteen planes in total at the time you stole these documents, eight of which were the faster model."

"And maybe they made more," Whistler suggested.

Or maybe they lost them, Jacob thought. He wondered where the Armageddon Brigade got their plane from in the first place. He did not want to dampen people's spirits, but he would not have been entirely surprised if they raided Rustport only to find it had already been raided before.

"We need volunteers," Rommond announced. "Ideally people who have flown before."

"Does being a passenger count?" Jacob quipped. The Skyshaker was enough experience of the air for him. Then again, the land was not all that much safer.

Cantro stepped forward. It seemed he was itching to get back into the sky.

"Well, Canto, you didn't exactly have a choice," Rommond said. "You're the best pilot we have."

"I don't want a choice," he said. "The sky's where I belong." He cast a forlorn glance towards the clouds.

"I want to fly," Whistler volunteered, holding up his hand.

"Well, he's a natural," Cantro said.

Rommond sighed. "Any other time, or any other mission, I'd say no. But this bomb won't distinguish between old and young, and I can't afford that distinction now." Jacob could tell that the general was not entirely comfortable with the fact that he had made that speech before with young lads he had sent to the front line, none of whom were now present.

"Count me in," Nissi said. She was Cantro's new trainee, daughter of one of the Treasury's wealthiest, and most eccentric, members, Count Alifred Willock. Everything about her was dark: her hair, her skin, and her clothes. She wore a tight corset, a short, frilled skirt over laced leggings, and a set of black pearls around her neck. She tied her hair up, as if she was about to set off right then and there. "I need the experience."

There was a remarkable silence after that, with no more raised hands.

"Is that it?" Rommond asked. "That's just four, myself included. This affects us all. I'm going to have to force some of you if you don't volunteer willingly. I'd rather not have to do that."

Jacob felt a weak nudge in his abdomen, and looked down to see Whistler's eager eyes. The smuggler looked back up again, only to feel a sharper nudge, and then another. It was probably paranoia, but he suddenly felt like everyone was staring at him, waiting for him to make a move.

"All right then," he said, holding up his hands.

"Eager as ever, I see," Rommond replied.

"Meh," Jacob blurted. "Think you'll have to take what you get at this stage."

"Indeed."

"Woo!" Whistler cheered, grabbing Jacob's arm.

"We can do flips and rolls and—"

Jacob felt nauseous already.

"That makes five," the general said. "I want at least three more, so we can use all of the monoplanes."

One of Leadman's burlier men, dubbed Armax, gave a nod. "I'll do it," he said, as if he was up for anything, "but I haven't flown one of those before. I'm more of a recon balloon kind of guy." He did not look it. He seemed like someone itching to be on the front lines. It must have been hell for him to have been kept back in Copperfort all those years.

"None of us have flown these before," Rommond said. "The controls are easy enough, I hear." He looked to Brooklyn, who stayed completely silent on the matter.

"Right then, Rommond, You can lead the aerial assault," Leadman said. "I'll organise the ground forces."

"There won't be any ground forces."

"What if you fail?"

"We won't."

"But what if you do?"

"Then it doesn't matter. There's only room for a Plan A here. We win, or we die."

Leadman scoffed.

"I'm leading another mission," Taberah unveiled. "We got word that Doctor Mudro was captured by the Regime, and we need him back for what I want to do."

"And what's that?" Leadman asked.

"Kill the Birth-masters."

"Now you're talking."

"You can join me," Taberah proposed. "It's a ground forces kind of mission."

"Great," Gregan said. "We can finally kill some demons."

A look from Rommond was enough for Taberah to round up and lead away the people joining her command. Tardo joined her, apologising profusely to Rommond as he went. "I'm really not good with heights!" he explained.

The remaining forces were very slim, and no one there was particularly eager to fly the experimental vehicles. It got so bad that Rommond's own lieutenants came up with a variety of excuses for why they could not fly. In the end, he could convince only one of them, Algan, to reluctantly volunteer, bringing their total number to seven.

"We'll have our work cut out for us," the general said.

"I hope they're not hard to master," Armax replied.

"For what we'll need to do, flying will be the easy part."

Chapter Four

PARTING PATHS

Taberah made her plans with the remaining ground forces, and set out to leave in the unwatched hours of the night. It was easier to slip out under the cover of darkness, not just because it was harder for the enemy to spot her, but because that way she did not have to cope with any painful farewells.

"No goodbye kiss?" Jacob asked, strolling up beside her as she packed the last of her things into a chest remarkably like the one that used to store his fortune. The lid was slightly ajar, so he could see there were no coils inside, nor clothes or keepsakes. Only weapons.

"How about a sting instead?" she said.

"If it's the sting of unending love and devotion, sure."

"Hardly."

Jacob kicked the box with his boot. "So, you were just going to take off?"

"I think it's better that way."

"I don't know. Us scorpions and spiders need to stick together."

"But scorpions and spiders are not really family."

He ran his hand through his shaggy hair. "Distant

cousins."

"Very distant."

"Doesn't have to be."

"It kind of does."

Jacob frowned. "Why do I get the feeling this is more than just a mission for you?"

"Because it is. It's my own little war within the war."

"I thought you only cared about the bigger picture."

She cocked her head. "This war is big enough."

Jacob kicked some sand away; there was always more to replace it. "You know ... did we ever really have a chance?"

She sighed. "Maybe in some other world."

"A demon world?"

She forced a smile. "Maybe there."

"Well, I guess this is goodbye then."

"I guess it is."

"What about Whistler?"

"What about him?"

"This doesn't just feel like a normal day or a normal week. Something's changed. The stakes are higher, and they were high before. What if some of us don't come back?"

"Then it *is* just a normal day and a normal week," she replied. "I've kind of gotten used to that. Most of us have. Maybe that's strange for a smuggler like you, but it's what we signed up to. Few of us expected to make it this far. None of us expect to make it all the way."

"Well, that's kind of grim."

"Well, that's the world we live in."

"So, what about Whistler then? Are you not going to say goodbye?"

She pursed her lips. "He's sleeping."

"Then wake him up, Taberah. Besides, no one's really sleeping well tonight."

"I can see that," she said, bowing her head.

"So?"

"I'll talk with him."

"Doesn't hurt to talk."

"Says the man who's all talk," she replied. "Sometimes it does."

"Hey, I walk the walk as well. Give me some credit."

She let out a sigh. "I guess you surprised me."

"I surprised myself."

"Speaking of surprises, I see you've gotten close with the nurse."

Jacob smirked. "What, are you jealous?"

"No," Taberah said coolly. "I'm concerned."

"Why? I'm a big boy."

"And you don't know what she is."

"I do," he replied. "Maran."

"So she taught you demon speech, did she?"

"It's easier to learn if you listen."

"I learned enough from them, Jacob. I still have the scars from those lessons."

"Well, I'm not really that interested in her," Jacob said. "You know who I'm interested in, who I've been interested in since this whole thing began. Pity it's all one way."

"Yeah," she said, nodding. "Pity."

"So, what have you got against Lorelai?" Jacob asked. "Apart from her being a big bad demon and all."

"Just watch your back with her," she said, before walking away.

Jacob thought about her words for a moment. As someone who had made a career out of watching people's backs, and stabbing them, he thought maybe she was on to something. Or maybe her words were just another blade.

Taberah stood outside the tent that Whistler slept in, feeling like she had no right to enter, no right to talk to him, or wake him, no right to even say goodbye. She knew she had not been a mother to him. She gave birth, but that was it. The mother in her died when Elizah died. There was no more love to give.

The curtain at the door shuddered in the wind, and through the periodic gap in it, she could see Whistler fast asleep, his hair a tangled mess, with the red of her own, and the brown of his father's. It was hard not to see Domas in him, even though he was completely unlike that man, unlike that demon.

The boy looked so peaceful in sleep. He gave a gentle purr, the prelude of the snoring he might give when he got older, when the boy in him would fade into the man, and it would be even more difficult to look upon him and not see Domas.

She had tried in her journal to write out the pain, to drown the memory of Domas in little splotches of ink. She had tried to write who she was, but found she could only write who she wanted to be. She had to focus on the bigger picture, because the smaller ones, the ones with Whistler in them, had his demon father in the background.

Domas gave her a child, but he took away her ability to love it.

Whistler woke up suddenly and wiped the sleep from his eyes. He had been having a pleasant dream, which was rare for him. He could not fully remember it, but he thought it had something to do with family.

He sat up and looked around the tent. He was used to sleeping rough, and sleeping on the move, and sleeping in so many different places. Everywhere was just a temporary refuge. He did not have a home.

He thought he heard someone outside.

"Who is it?" he asked.

"It's me," his mother said. The normal forcefulness of her voice was restrained, though it almost sounded like she had to force that restraint.

"Oh," Whistler uttered unintentionally, trying to mask the disappointment.

There was a brief pause.

"Can I come in?"

"I guess."

The curtain parted, and Taberah stepped in hesitantly. To anyone else watching at that moment, they would have recognised where Whistler's own perpetual hesitation came from. And yet, his mother was not hesitant in anything else.

"I just wanted to ... talk," she said, standing awkwardly by the entrance. Perhaps she expected him to tell her to get out. Part of him expected he might still do.

"Why?" he asked.

"Why?" she repeated, showing the same surprise that he showed about her presence there.

"I mean … why talk? Why now?"

"I know we haven't had a great relationship, Brogan." She approached closer, like a predator stalking its prey. "I'm sorry."

Whistler pouted and shrugged his shoulders. He knew he could not just say *It's okay*. It was not okay. He could not lie like that, even to make her feel better, even though part of him really wanted to. The part of him that did not feel better always stopped him.

"The war may be over soon," she said. He doubted that. He was born in the war. The war was his life. He wondered if even the Regime disappeared, if the fighting would not just start somewhere else, with someone else. He had fourteen years to try to understand "why," and he was still trying.

"I have a new mission," Taberah added, when he did not give a reply. "I thought maybe … you and me … we could create a pleasant memory—just in case."

"Just in case?"

"I'm not sure what will happen. I know I wasn't there for you, Brogan. I might not be there for you in the future either. I might not be here for anyone."

"No," Whistler said, shaking his head. "Why are you saying this?"

"Because I'm not sure I belong here."

Whistler furrowed his brow. "Doesn't everyone feel like that?"

"Perhaps," Taberah said. "But I haven't felt like

this in a long time. I was writing the story of my life in my diary, and I feel like now my story is coming to an end. I just want our last chapter together to be a little better than the ones before. I know it's my fault the others weren't. If only I tried a little harder. If only I could see past … *him*."

A tear rolled down Whistler's cheek. He could feel it, caressing him, like she never did. "But you can still try now," he said. "Can't you?"

"I don't think I can, Brogan. I don't think I can."

Another tear followed, and it felt a little colder than the last. "But I thought … maybe you and Jacob … and me. No?"

She gave a teary smile, like someone remembering a pleasant dream. Then she shook her head. "No. I'm still chasing ghosts. I can't chase anything else."

Whistler's lip trembled, and his voice was hoarse and broken. "Why won't you fight for me, mom? Why do you fight for everything else? Am I not good enough?"

He could see her struggle with her own tears, in case they doused the flames. "You're good enough," she said. "You're too good. Way too good for me. I don't deserve you. You would have been better off with someone else. You still will be."

"But there *is* no one else," he said. "You're my mom. I don't *want* anyone else."

He reached his hand out to hers. She involuntarily recoiled her own, then brought her hand back to gently hold his. Yet she would not look him in the eyes. Not in Domas' eyes. She was always chasing ghosts, and though he was gone, the dead still haunted her.

"I wish it could be different," Taberah said. "I can't make it up to you. I can't make amends. All I can do is be honest with you."

She held his arms and bowed her head towards him, until her forehead rested against his, until their tears joined together in a little pool below them. It was the closest they had been in a long time, and yet she still felt very far away.

"Don't weep for me," she said. "Don't weep for us."

She started to withdraw, but he grabbed her hand with both of his. She glanced at him, then looked away, before pulling away from him. He held her hand for a moment, but she did not hold his. His grip was weak, and her fingers slid through his, until—as she was only weeks before—he was holding nothing.

Chapter Five

THE RUST ROAD

Jacob found Lorelai patching up Rommond's back in the medical tent. He cringed at the sight of all the criss-crossing scars, many still bleeding. Brooklyn was there too, grimacing at the sight.

"Hell," Jacob said. "I see you're a dab hand at the old self-flagellation."

"Well, we all strive for perfection," Rommond grumbled, clearly irritated at anyone seeing him without his shirt, coat and medals on. They were pristinely displayed on a nearby mannequin.

"I'm surprised you let anyone patch you up," Jacob said.

"I had to make him," Brooklyn explained.

"And just as well you did," Lorelai added, casting away a bloodied cloth. "I've never seen such terrible sewing before in my life. No wonder you boys don't do your own trouser legs."

"Well, you try sewing up your own back," the general snapped, pulling away from her needle. "Are we done?"

"Not really," she said, but he was already buttoning up his shirt.

"He is stubborn," Brooklyn pointed out.

Rommond shook his head. "It isn't stubbornness if you're right."

"I guess you're right then," Jacob said.

The general gave him a sardonic smile. "Let's go. We should set out as soon as possible."

"Sure, just give me a minute."

"A minute," Rommond insisted, as if he would accept nothing more. He linked Brooklyn's arm and left the tent.

Lorelai started to wrap up her bandages. She cast a glance at Jacob, as if she was surprised he was still there. He thought her job must have felt a little unrewarding. Those she successfully patched up left just as quickly. Those who stayed were dead.

"So, I suppose you're not coming on the road trip," he said.

"I don't think I'd be any help on one of those flying machines. Besides, there are still many people injured from the battle of the Iron Wall."

"You mean the Landquaker."

She smiled at him. "It's all the same."

"Yeah, I guess it is. Well, until the next cut or bruise." He gave her a mock salute, then left to join the others.

Rommond spared little time in setting out. He already felt they wasted enough with planning, and yet the master planner knew no other method. He divided his pilots into two trucks, keeping Jacob, Algan and Whistler with him. Armax led the other team, at Leadman's insistence, with Cantro and Nissi.

Wisdom would have had them take another

way, but there were few options left for the weakened Resistance, and so they decided on the Rust Road, an old trading route that was abandoned for good reason. There the carcasses of machines piled up on either side like metal cliffs, and it was not the erosion of weather that ate away at them, but something far more mischievous, and far more deadly.

"The Clockwork Commune," Jacob mused. "Yet another one of those names I thought belonged to the fairy tales." He shifted uneasily in his leather seat.

"So you're starting to believe?" Rommond asked, sitting perfectly still.

"I'm wishing I could remain incredulous."

"They're friendly though, aren't they?" Whistler wondered. He rested his chin on the back of Jacob's seat, peering over his shoulder at the path ahead. He did not budge at the mention of the clockwork constructs either. *Maybe wonder trumps fear*, Jacob thought.

Rommond scoffed. "If you have no metal."

"Shame you got that gold tooth then," Jacob quipped.

"Trust me, Jacob, they'll rip through that ribcage of yours to see if you have any gold in you too—especially if you arrive in a vehicle. That's as much a 'come get me' cry as any other."

The truck purred a little louder, a cry of its own.

"Remind me again why we're going this way?" Jacob asked.

"This is the quiet road." Still, the general spent a lot of time loading guns. The dashboard was starting to get very cluttered with them.

"Yeah, for good reason, it sounds like."

"All roads carry risks. This is the only one unpoliced by the Regime. If we are to get to Rustport with ease, then this is our only option. We threw everything we had at the Landquaker, and even that is now destroyed. Had we that gun, we could have stormed Rustport by rail. Now … we sneak in."

Jacob perked up. "Sounds like a smuggling route."

He could see Whistler smiling knowingly at him from the rear-view mirror.

"Precisely," the general said. "Maybe you'll be useful after all."

"After all?" Jacob scoffed. "I think I've been pretty useful so far."

"So far," Whistler jeered.

"Cheeky." He paused. "You know, it's kind of funny."

"What is?" Rommond asked, holding a shotgun shell up for inspection. He seemed unhappy at the tiny imperfections in it.

"That we're now trying to save the Iron Emperor."

"We're not trying to save *him*."

"Yeah, but that'll be the net result of what we do, when we stop the Worldwaker."

"I like your confidence," Algan said from the back seat. He was a quiet type, one of Rommond's unsung lieutenants. He did what he was told, and got people to do what they were told. The general had a lot of people like that. Jacob was not one of them.

"Something tells me he won't appreciate the gesture," Jacob continued.

"I could have told you that," Rommond said.

"You kind of pity them," Jacob said. "Our 'enemy.'"

"You might, but I don't." The general had a lot of polished weapons to prove it.

"What's there to pity?" Algan added, reinforcing Rommond's view.

"Well, they didn't really sign up for this," Jacob said. He could really empathise with that. "It was all the Iron Emperor. He came and conquered them. Conquering is all he's about. It's even on the coils we use."

"Is that what the nurse told you?" Rommond asked. "If he conquered them, they let him. He came with gifts and promises, and they voted for him willingly. The Devil did not storm office. He hid his horns and was elected."

"So you know they're not really demons then. You know their history."

"I know enough," Rommond said, giving his revolver another scrub. "We always demonise our adversaries. I'm a general, Jacob. This is part of the propaganda that helps us win a war. Except in the case of the marans, what they've done, the path they've chosen, is inherently demonic—so they demonised themselves."

"And what about us?"

"What about us?"

"Well, we're not exactly angels either."

"We don't have to be to be good."

Jacob furrowed his brow. "I suppose you're right."

The day wore on, and Rommond scrambled into the back to take a nap, insisting that he would be on watch for the duration of their time on the Rust Road—a promise that was not encouraging. Algan followed suit, and both were snoring in no time.

Whistler sat in the front with the smuggler, hugging his legs and resting his chin on his knees. He kept well enough away from Rommond's arsenal. He seemed distracted, looking neither at the weapons nor the road ahead, his mouth formed into a perpetual pout.

"Are you okay?" Jacob asked.

Whistler was startled from his daze. "Yeah. Why?"

"You seem a little … I don't know … distracted."

Whistler bit his lip and shrugged. "It's nothing," he said. He was not a good liar. Jacob decided not to press the issue.

"What was your mom like?" the boy asked after a brief pause.

"My mom?"

"Yeah."

"Eh, she was nice. You know, I kind of don't remember her that well. I was a kid when she died. My last memories of her were in the workhouse. We didn't really get to be family there."

"Oh." Whistler scrunched his mouth, contorting it from side to side. "Sorry."

"Well, it's not your fault."

"I know. It's just … that's what we're supposed to say, right?"

"Yeah, I suppose."

"If the war ended today … what would you do? Where would you go?"

"Hell," Jacob said. "I haven't thought that far ahead. Have you?"

Whistler shrugged. "A little."

"Who knows what the future holds? There's really no point in worrying about it."

"I guess."

"Well then, what would you do?"

"I don't know."

"Seems we're in the same boat then."

"While we have a reason to paddle together."

Jacob raised an eyebrow. "What's this about?"

Whistler shrugged again. It seemed he shrugged not because he did not have an answer, but because he was afraid to tell it. "Will you go back to smuggling?"

"Probably," Jacob said. "Don't think I'd be much good at anything else. Can you imagine me as a farmer? Or a miner? Don't think I could do an honest day's work."

Whistler forced a chuckle. "Yeah, I guess so."

Jacob frowned. "You're supposed to say *No, Jacob, I think you'd do a great job at any of those*."

The boy gave the faintest of smiles. "If … when this is all over," he said. "Can … can we still be friends?"

"Of course," Jacob said, putting his arm around Whistler's shoulder. "Buddies for life. Sure, who else'd I get to squash into all the small places? Master and apprentice smuggler." He held his hand out, waving it across the darkening sky, as if he could paint the words there. "Look out, world!"

* * *

As dusk set in, they set out along the Canopy Trail, where the traders of old used to gather to sell their wares. Scraps of fabric from pavilions, gazebos, tents and other canopies still clung to the periodic metal poles that littered the landscape, the sand-laced material clattering in the fierce breeze. It was a desolate scene, but the people of Altadas had gotten pretty used to desolation.

As the darkness deepened, the sky was streaked with veins of red, the last low beats of a dying sun. Against this scarlet canopy, the hulk of the Rust Road's twin peaks stood tall, mountains of metal, unnaturally jagged. Their sharp pinnacles pierced the sky, and Jacob could not help but wonder if that explained the blood there.

It did not take long before they fell fully under the shadow of those sentinels, and what fading glimmers of sunlight peaked through only accentuated the form. Thousands of vehicles were piled hundreds of feet high on either side, a tangled mess of metal. The only thing that was abundantly clear was that the vehicles had been thoroughly scavenged, and all that was left was the empty shells. Anything of use or value was removed, and forcibly so. Everything else, the useless skin, was left to rot.

Armax drove behind, dimming his lights. Jacob followed suit. They needed just enough to see, not to be seen.

Jacob got ready to wake the general, as requested, but he found Rommond already stirring, as if the shadows of the junk yard had invaded his sleep. He came back to the waking world with that recognisable grim determination in his eyes, suggesting he might have slain demons and destroyed clockwork constructs as he snored.

He ushered Whistler to change places. "Let me go in front, there's a good chap."

Whistler closed his eyes in the back, and Algan rolled over in his sleep. He did what he was told, but the general had not told him to wake up yet.

As Rommond adjusted his uniform, Jacob studied the iron graveyard, where every vehicle was its own gravestone. He drove slowly through, as if he was afraid to wake the dead. That was not it though. The general made it clear that they should fear the living.

"You know, you probably should melt these wrecks down and make some coils with the iron," Jacob suggested.

"Oh, we tried that," Rommond replied. "Back in the early days of the war. The Regime copped on quick and changed the coils to make them impossible to replicate."

"Really? I never noticed a difference. Have you got an original?"

"Sure," Rommond said. He flicked the coil over to Jacob.

Jacob inspected it between glances at the winding road, but did not see anything unfamiliar. The general must have noticed, because he flicked another coil over.

"This is the new type, the ones we haven't been able to copy."

Jacob compared them. They were both made the

same: an iron coil flattened, and stamped on one side with the image of the Iron Emperor, surrounded by his maran slogan.

"So, what am I looking for?"

Rommond smiled. "That's what I said when I was shown this for the first time. Tilt the new one."

Jacob did just that, and watched as the Iron Emperor's gawking eyes followed him.

"Now tilt the old one."

Jacob tried it, but the eyes did not follow him.

"That's an old painter's trick, right?" Jacob asked.

"Not the way they do it here," Rommond explained. "And I know, because I used to paint, and when I saw this, I tried my hand at painting the Iron Emperor as if he was staring straight at me. His eyes follow, sure, but look again."

Jacob tilted the newer coil once more, and then he saw it. Depending on whether it was tilted back or forward, or side to side, the Iron Emperor's eyes did not just continue their eternal staring—they changed colour.

"Hell," Jacob said. "How come I never noticed that before?"

"Too busy spending them, perhaps," the general said.

"So, you couldn't copy this?"

"We tried, but we couldn't get the eyes to shift colours, at least not in the same way. Our fakes were spotted swiftly in several trial trades, so we abandoned the idea. Project Ironeyes, we called it. Such a pity we were never successful, as that's when I had to go begging to the Treasury for loans, and I'm not much of a begging man."

"You should have put me in charge of Project Ironeyes," Jacob mused. "You never know what I might have done."

"Well, you weren't Resistance material back then, now, were you?" Rommond asked. "And we never know what you might still do."

The trucks drove with very little light. Rommond revealed that many in the Clockwork Commune were virtually blind, and could not detect the dimmest light. Jacob was not so sure about that, but he had paid little attention to the whispers and rumours he heard from other smugglers. The chink of coils drowned out everything else.

It was not just the light that was turned down. Anything inessential was turned off. The trucks chugged along at the slowest of speeds, barely rolling forward at all. It was so quiet that they could hear the gentle crunch of the tires against the earth.

"Is it true?" Jacob asked, when the silence got to him. He glanced at Whistler to make sure he was still asleep. He felt like he was asking about a nightmare.

"Is what true?" Rommond asked in turn.

"That they killed their maker."

"I never got close enough to ask them."

"Well, you have your sources, right?"

Rommond gave the slightest of shrugs. "I don't really care how they began. I care what they do now. And now they're a nuisance."

"Kind of like the Armageddon Brigade."

The general grumbled. "Kind of like you."

The sudden sound of scurrying seized Jacob's attention.

"What's that?" he asked.

Rommond slowly raised his index finger to his lip to shush him. He reached with his other hand for his gun.

They heard what sounded like the ticking of a clock, yet faster, a mechanical heartbeat. Then they heard it again from somewhere else, and again, until it seemed that there were many little beats, some in the same rhythm, others faster, and others slower. There were at least a dozen independent noises out there, all joined together in a commune of sound.

In the rear-view mirror, Jacob saw Whistler stirring from his slumber, wiping his eyes. He also saw something stepping out onto the road behind them.

Chapter Six

AVALANCHE

"Step on it!" Rommond ordered. "They know we're here."

Jacob revved the engine and stomped on the accelerator. He could hear the other truck following suit, thundering along just inches behind them, close enough that he could see Armax's eager eyes in the mirror.

The trucks hurtled along the Rust Road, clipping the butchered ruins of vehicles that jutted out of the towering iron walls on either side. The trail twisted and turned, sometimes sharply, forcing Jacob to turn even sharper, and almost topple the truck in the process.

Behind, in the darkness, the ticking and shuffling grew. The Clockwork Commune were made of many things, and some of them were steamtruck wheels and landship tracks. They salvaged speed, and used it to help them salvage everything else.

The other truck pulled up beside Jacob's, bumping into the side. Armax grinned at him, hunched his shoulders, and pressed his head closer to the wheel, as if he thought that would help him gain speed.

"He thinks it's a race," Jacob said.

"It is," Rommond replied, "but not between us."

The Commune gained on them, a mangled mass of rotating wheels and cogs, and scurrying limbs that were most in need of oiling. The sound was deafening, like a thousand factories chugging away at once, each part of the machinery competing to drown out the next.

Armax sped by, a distraction from the chase, and Jacob took the next corner too early, slicing into one of the outcropping cars. The force of the impact spun the truck around and rocked it on its weathered wheels, but it also dislodged the car from its cage, and left the one above it dangling precariously and creaking loudly.

The people in the truck had barely caught their breath, and Jacob had barely reorientated himself, when they heard the groan of the metal grow louder.

Rommond shook his head. "God no."

The dangling car slid down a notch, then caught in the torn metal of another. This, in turn, set the next vehicle off, and the shifting and creaking spread from one to another like a set of iron dominoes—a set which spanned the entire Rust Road.

"Drive!" Rommond screamed.

Yet despite Jacob's every effort, the truck would not move.

"I'm trying!" he shouted back.

He pressed the accelerator with even more force, and he could feel and hear the wheels of the steamtruck spin, but it barely rocked in place.

Whistler hung out one of the windows, like a dangling car of his own. "There's something stuck there," he cried. He opened the door and hopped outside, where he could see what looked like part of a car door wedged between the axle of the front wheels, the other end buried deep in the sand. "I see it!" he said, and tried to pull it out, but he did not have the strength to remove it.

Algan and Rommond joined him, and even they struggled to dislodge the piece. "Reverse up," he called to Jacob. "Reverse up!"

Whistler yanked on Rommond's coat and pointed with a shaking hand to the path they had come from. There they could see several dozen misshapen figures racing up towards them, a horde of steel, waving jagged bits of metal, salivating oil in the search for more.

They freed the truck just in time, leaping back inside and slamming the door, even as a little metal hand tried to grab it. Jacob fired up the engine, and the vehicle sprang forward, sending a burst of smoke at the attackers.

Yet this swift motion also set off another, for the dangling vehicles that made up the metal wall to their left began to topple. One by one, then a dozen at a time, the cars and trucks, the landships and airships began to fall. An avalanche of parts came tumbling down, crushing many of the Clockwork Commune.

But the mountain spanned for miles, and so the avalanche spread, threatening the stability of the entire trail. What the clockwork creatures had spent a lifetime accumulating and arranging in a precarious work of art, the Resistance had spent an artless moment pulling down.

As the steamtruck thundered across the Rust Road, the collapsing cliff followed. That it only followed was their blessing for now, but the threat of a curse grew all the time, for the vehicles further ahead began to rock in place from the force of the tumbling metal tide. It seemed that at any moment the Great Iron War would be over for them, and they would become part of the road that they travelled, just another iron slab in the pavement, just another iron brick in the wall.

Then something fell from the wall, striking the truck and sending it skidding to the side. Jacob regained control, but by the time he did they realised it was not falling debris—something leapt at them and landed on the roof. They could hear it walking above.

Jacob pointed up and pursed his lips.

Rommond reached for the shotgun in the front.

Then a spinning saw cut through the roof at the back where Whistler and Algan sat. They screamed and recoiled, ducking low in their seats as the metal canopy tore open.

Rommond fired at the clockwork construct, but it was quick, and the moving of the vehicle disturbed his normally good aim. The mechanical monster was a collection of arms, with three heads, each with a gigantic eye, making it look like some kind of iron spider.

It continued to saw through the roof while it reached one of its claws inside. Whistler and Algan kicked at the metal limb, while Rommond fired a second shot, blowing off the saw-wielding limb, which spun off into the still tumbling pile of junk beside them, where it continued to eat through the husks of vehicles, further destabilising the wall.

The clockwork creature had no more limbs to cut, but it had many left to grab, and it forced part of its torso through the gape in the roof and reached out to Whistler and Algan, gripping them by the legs and tearing through their clothes.

Rommond tried to reload, but he dropped the shell as Jacob took the next corner hard, partly because he had no option to slow down with the approaching avalanche, and partly in an attempt to dislodge their arachnid attacker.

Up ahead, Armax's truck slowed a little, and Nissi smashed the back window with the butt of her gun. She aimed the rifle through and fired, but the bullet missed the monster and shattered the windscreen of Jacob's truck. He shook the splintered glass from his hair.

"Hell, that's not helping," he said.

Rommond finished loading, fired, cocked, and fired again, tearing off two more of the creature's mechanical limbs. By now, however, it had hauled Whistler upside down and was beginning to pull him, screaming, through the torn roof.

Algan grabbed hold of Whistler and tried desperately to stop him being pulled outside. He bashed at the metal claws, but their grip only tightened.

Rommond struck the nearest claw with the butt of the shotgun, then took out his pistol and unloaded all five bullets into the wiry sinews, until it could no longer clasp anything. Whistler fell back down, but this time the creature seized Algan and pulled him halfway through the gap. Whistler clambered up and grabbed his leg, but he did not have the strength to pull him back inside.

Rommond scrambled into the back seat, reaching up to Algan's disappearing feet. He grabbed a hold, then pushed his torso through the hole to fight the mechanical creature. At that point, just as he had a firm grasp on one of its remaining limbs, a bullet cruised by, fired from the truck ahead, severing the limb and knocking the creature, along with Algan, off the roof.

"Algan!" Whistler cried.

Rommond angrily threw the iron limb aside, looked ahead to Nissi, and back at Algan as he was hauled away by the mangled monster. He hopped back inside and climbed into the front passenger seat.

"We have to go back," Jacob said, pushing hard on the breaks.

"Leave him!" Rommond ordered, slamming his foot down on Jacob's, forcing the truck back into motion. "There's no saving him now."

As they drove on, they heard the screams and cries of Algan behind them, carried by the sneering wind. Though Jacob kept his eyes on the road ahead, from the mirrors he could see the Clockwork Commune ripping Algan apart, shredding him in their search for metal. That they were quick was perhaps a mercy, but Jacob could not help but think that they were anything but merciful.

They drove on in silence, and yet the Rust Road made all the noises for them. Algan's screams died off, and the ticking died down, but the creaking and crunching of falling metal continued until they passed through the final stretch of the Rust Road.

The avalanche was over, and the path behind was sealed. The mountain had moved, and from the sounds of creaking metal, it was still moving. A lonely tyre bounced down and rolled by the steamtruck, as if to escape the tumble. Jacob halted the vehicle, and it jerked to a stop, rolling up beside Armax.

Amidst the howling wind and their heavy breathing, there were no sounds of ticking clocks, just the groaning of the scrapyard wall behind them.

"Well," Jacob panted. "I guess we're not going back that way."

Chapter Seven

RIDDLES IN RUINS

Taberah's team rolled out with just two vehicles, her own unarmed warwagon, the Silver Ghost, and Leadman's newly-retrofitted landship, recently delivered from the workshops of Copperfort, with a massive bulldozer blade attached to the front. It flattened the uneven sands as it went, making the journey smoother for them all.

They headed due east into Regime territory, passing over the broken and unguarded track of the Iron Wall, into part of Altadas that was drier and hotter than the rest. They saw no aeroplanes there, nor landships, nor even a fortress to bar the way. No one had prepared for the Iron Wall to fall.

The Silver Ghost halted near a ruined building, one of the old burial places of the bygone dynasty to which the Treasury were the living heirs. No one went there now to pay their respects. Homage was paid with iron in the coffers of Blackout.

"You be safe now," Taberah said to Brooklyn as they stepped outside. "Are you sure you don't want anyone to come with you?"

"This is my mission," Brooklyn said. "You have your own, and you need army for it."

"I need more than soldiers."

"Then save doctor."

"I'll try."

Leadman's landship pulled up close, with the general popping through the hatch.

"Not to press you," he said, "but don't we have people to kill?"

Brooklyn nodded to Taberah, and she nodded back. *If only all goodbyes could be so easy*, she thought.

Brooklyn turned, then froze, staring ahead at the ruins.

"There is someone out there."

"Give them a volley," Leadman told the gunner below.

The turret fired, and part of the building exploded. They heard a frenzied voice inside. When the dust settled a little, out popped a chequered handkerchief tied to a gnarly stick, which was waved about frantically like a flag of surrender.

"Nothing like a landship to weed out the rats," Leadman said. "Throw out your weapons," he shouted to the figure inside the ruins.

"W-w-well, I would," the man stammered, "but I d-don't have any."

Taberah thought that the voice was familiar, and the stammer even moreso.

"We don't believe you," the general said. "Maybe we can send another shell to investigate."

"I s-s-swear!" the man cried, running out to them, hands waving madly in the air.

"Stop!" Taberah told the general. She shook her head. "I know him."

"You do?"

"He's my brother."

Out stepped Alex Cotten. He was middle-aged, but there was something about him that suggested he was always like that, that perhaps he was even born that age. Everything was very twee about him, from his mannerisms to his dress. His clothing was quaint, mostly tan in colour, with a chequered shirt, a tweed coat and waistcoat, and a polka dot bow tie, which was perhaps the most exciting thing about him. His small round, brass glasses gave him an air of intellectualism, but the way he wore his brimmed straw hat, slightly tilted to the side, gave him an air of the buffoon. He was the antithesis of Taberah, with her bold dress and bold colours, and bold personality.

"That's history you're destroying there!" the man shrieked hysterically, pointing back to the ruins while still keeping both hands in the air.

"Well, the sooner you come fully out," Leadman said, "the sooner we can shoot you instead of those ruins."

Alex stepped forward, glancing back disapproving at the crumbled building. It took a while for him to notice Taberah standing in front of him.

"What are you doing here?" she asked.

"D-d-dearest me," he stammered. "It's you!"

"You say that like it's a bad thing."

"Not at all. I'm j-j-just … surprised, is all."

His stammers came and went, depending on how excited he was, and it seemed that in those ruins he was very excited indeed. He struggled with his words, as if he had not been around others in quite some time. Perhaps he talked to the statues in the tomb's chambers, the statues that would not judge him or mock his speech, and maybe they merely listened, or maybe they talked back.

"I should have expected to find you lurking in some ruins," Taberah said.

"Well, yes."

"I guess this one takes after your mother," Leadman commented. "Margey Cotten. A fine woman for a bookworm." He looked disapprovingly at Alex. "I suppose you're more of a sandworm yourself."

"Eh, a p-p-pleasure to meet you," Alex replied, adjusting his wide-brimmed glasses. He held his hand up towards the general, but Leadman did not shake it.

"I'm glad one of you followed in the footsteps of your father," Leadman said, glancing at Taberah. "Just a pity it had to be the girl."

"I'm glad one of these days you'll be dead," she replied. "Just a pity it's not sooner."

Brooklyn seemed awkward between them. "I will let you get on with your mission. I must complete my own. It is long journey ahead, and lonely one."

"Where are you off to?" Alex asked him.

"Dunedale."

"Dunedale? I know the way, if you need a g-guide."

"Guide would be useful," Brooklyn acknowledged. He had not exactly mapped the route when he was captured and dragged through Regime territory.

"It was good to see you again, Alex," Taberah said.

"And you!"

They parted ways, Alex scrambling through the broken ruins, and Brooklyn following. They were the symbols of the old world, an archaeologist and a tribesman, wandering on foot, while the great landship and iron transport spat smoke and steam as they rolled away.

Chapter Eight

RUSTPORT

At the end of the Rust Road, neither truck stopped for long, for fear of the Worldwaker ahead, and the Clockwork Commune behind. They continued until the rising sun highlighted their destination.

"I see it!" Whistler cried. "Look!" He prodded Jacob's shoulder, as if he needed prodding to see the metal towers appearing on the horizon.

"Rustport," Rommond said ominously. "Either our haven, or our end."

The city of Rustport rose from the sandy haze before them, a city of towers and chimneys, of scrap metal turned into housing. It sat on the edge of the ocean, the Last Sea, and over time it stretched out over the sea itself, with a mixture of wooden and metal walkways, some fixed deep into the earth, others floating, and others still sinking and rising as the need came for them.

It was a vibrant city, a mariner's home, with many ships docked, and others docking. There was the smell of salt sea air, mixed with the stink of fish and the musk of industry. It was a city of labourers and tradesmen, with no room for pretence, and so there was zero presence from the Treasury there, whose members would not have been able to bear the stench.

The tracks of the Iron Wall fed into the city, and it was the protection of the Landquaker that stopped it from falling to the Regime for so long. It was that same protection that kept the Resistance from retaking the port when the demons gained control of the railway gun. It meant that Rustport had very little in other defences, which the Regime felt were needed more at Landlock up north. Yet it was likely only a matter of time before reinforcements were drafted in from further east.

The trucks halted at the outskirts of the city, where workers passed them by without batting an eyelid. It did not matter if the Resistance or the Regime was in the city. They had work to do.

"So then," Jacob said. "Do we trade in our uniforms for fisherman's overalls?"

Rommond rolled his eyes at him.

"Seriously though," the smuggler added. "What's our plan here?"

"We'll simply propose a truce," the general said.

"Maybe I've spent too long in their uniform, but I can't see them going for it."

"We'll have to bluff our way."

"Now you're talking my language," Jacob said, "but then you did know that I'm a gambling man. So, what's the bluff?"

"That if they don't agree, we'll take the city by force."

"Ah," Jacob said, less confident now. "You know, it's a bit easier to fake it when you're not showing your cards." He gestured to the handful of people they had.

"The Regime knows that I never play all my cards up front," Rommond reminded him.

"Yeah, but this time you are."

"And that's the bluff. That's the card I never played before."

Jacob sucked air through his teeth. "All right then. But … what if they call your bluff?"

Rommond gave the slightest of smiles. "Then we take the city by force."

A truck pulled up, flanked by two of the Regime's box-shaped landships. Out stepped a short and rotund commander, crudely attired, and a tall woman in a long, flowing purple dress, hanging out of his arm, and looking remarkably out of place.

"Well, well, well," the commander said, clapping his hands together and rubbing them briskly, as if he had just won a prize. He had the thick, common accent of Rustport, but a glance from Whistler revealed that he was most definitely maran. "If it isn't Edward Rommond himself."

Rommond gave a slight nod. "If it isn't … sorry, I don't know who *you* are."

The commander could not hide his irritation. "Ovunan Trokus," he said. "Commander, that is."

"I can see your rank well enough. Where's your General?"

"I'm in command here."

"Good," Rommond said. "You look like an easy kill."

Trokus gritted his teeth. "You know, you shouldn't

provoke when there are so few of you."

Armax folded his arms and puffed his chest.

"As you well know, Mr. Trokus," Rommond replied, "the Resistance has never needed numbers."

"There's a first time for everything, Mr. Rommond. Maybe this is it."

Rommond raised the index finger of his left hand. "But you're not thinking this through. You didn't think we'd come here in so few numbers if we didn't have a plan, did you?"

Trokus' grin faded into the flabs on his face.

"The Landquaker is on the way," Rommond said.

"But it was derailed."

"That it was," the general acknowledged. "But, as you know ... Brooklyn's back."

The mention of Brooklyn crushed whatever sliver of a smile remained on Trokus' face.

"Darlin'," the lady crooned. "Perhaps I should go back inside."

"Hang on a minute," Trokus said through his clenched teeth.

"If you think I won't shoot you in front of your wife," Rommond said, "you're very much mistaken."

The guards pointed their guns at the general, but he did not flinch. In fact, he showed an element of boredom at the display, as if he had seen it all a thousand times before. He had.

Rommond gestured dismissively to the guards. "None of *this* matters. Right now, all that matters is *you* ... and the bullet meant for you. You see, I'm not a religious man, but I do believe in fate. Your fate. I believe it's in my hands."

This is some bluff, Jacob thought, and yet he was not entirely sure it was. In many ways, everything Rommond said was true. But there was a lot of cold iron truth in the guns pointed at them as well.

"You're talking a lot," Trokus said, "for a man who likes to shoot first."

Trokus' wife gripped his hand tightly. Rommond saw it, and Jacob saw it too.

"Well," the general said, "words are our weapons tonight, and we need them, because there is a bigger threat out there than either of us. You've probably heard of the Armageddon Brigade and Project Ironending."

"Can't say that I have."

Rommond cocked his head. "Let's pretend that you haven't then. I cancelled the project, but the Brigade continued it. And now it's done."

Trokus' worry was evident.

"They're already in the air," Rommond continued, "so you can pretend that doesn't mean the clock is ticking, but even now we might already be too late. Ironhold looks like the target, but the beauty of the bomb is that it changes everything, even for those who survive—if any survive. We call each other monsters, but there's one real monster up there in the sky."

"You don't need to convince me any more."

Maybe this might work after all, Jacob thought.

"But we'll need approval," Trokus added.

And ... there it goes tumbling down.

"Then get approval," Rommond said. "But don't take long in getting it. A new age is approaching, and its advent might make us pray to go back to the days of the trenches. Once the Worldwaker goes off, we will never be able to sleep again."

Chapter Nine

CABARET

While the Regime forces contacted headquarters, and awaited approval for a temporary truce by the Iron Emperor himself, the Resistance team were "welcomed" into Rustport, ushered along at gunpoint, and led into a murky bar with flashing lights that read: Club Crimson.

"We'll need your weapons," Trokus said.

Rommond stood firm. "Not a chance."

"We'll give you the bullets," Armax taunted. "A whole belly full."

"Now, *that* I'm fine with," the general said, "if you are, Mr. Trokus."

Trokus grumbled and let them inside, guns and all.

The light was low, which made the shadows long. Had Jacob and company not been painfully aware that they were surrounded by Regime forces, those menacing shadows would have reminded them. There was something about a maran shadow that seemed different to a human one.

Maybe I'm just imagining it, Jacob thought, *but hell, they do look a little demonic.*

"Do you always bring your good lady with you to

dangerous situations?" Rommond asked.

Trokus grunted. "Do you always bring yours?" he retorted, nodding towards Jacob.

The smuggler snorted. "Who said I was the wife?"

They sat at a table in the centre of the club, within eyeshot and gunshot of everyone else. It was not the location Rommond or Jacob would have picked, but they were forced to indulge in Trokus' demonstration of Regime hospitality. Jacob stared uneasily at the drink he was given. He was very thirsty, but very suspicious too. Armax seemed to have no such suspicions. He downed his glass without qualm.

The background music stopped sharp, as if the pianist's fingers had been chopped off. The curtains pulled open, and the spotlight turned on. Jacob shifted uneasily. Spotlights were not his thing. Too many people died in them. He felt like even in the darkness of the audience, there was another spotlight on them.

Trokus' wife, Arlesei, stepped onto the stage and grabbed the microphone. As melodic as the piano was, her voice outmatched it in every way, both in beauty and volume. She gave a spell-binding performance of an old seafarer's song, a local tune, slow as the endless erosion of the sea, and the sound chipped away at even the hardest of hearts. Then she ended with a quick ditty, which was not local at all, and was clearly a soldier's song devised by the Regime. The crowd chanted and banged their mugs and glasses on the tables, and the only ones who did not join in stood out awkwardly at Trokus' table.

"She's quite a women, eh?" Trokus said.

"Quite," Rommond replied.

"'Course, you don't go in for that kind o' thing, do you?" Trokus said with a grin.

Rommond did not so much as twitch.

The crowd cheered and whistled, and there might have been a shout of "encore," but it was made in the maran tongue. Rommond gave a polite clap, which Jacob and Whistler matched, albeit a little more enthusiastically.

You cheer the performance or you become the performance, Jacob thought.

They watched as Arlesei stepped off the stage and strolled straight past the salivating soldiers with their outstretched hands, to where a teenage boy and young girl sat. She embraced them both fondly, kissing each on the cheek, before sitting down with them.

"What?" Trokus said. "You thought she was just a trophy wife? Shame on you. She's a wonderful mother. Couldn't ask for more. I already got more than I deserve in life." He rapped his fingers off his chest. "I got family."

"So I see," Rommond replied.

"And you didn't a minute ago. Well, General, maybe you shouldn't be so quick to judge."

Rommond stifled a sigh and said nothing.

"This one," Trokus said, gesturing towards Whistler. "I know he's not yours, Rommond." He looked intently at Jacob. "He your kid?"

Jacob glanced at Whistler and smiled.

Trokus held his hands out. "What's that supposed to be? You going to be rude or answer my question?"

"Not by blood," Jacob said.

"So no then," Trokus said, and Whistler frowned. "You got any family, soldier?" Trokus asked Jacob.

"Not really." *And not really a soldier*, he thought.

"Not really? You either do or you don't."

Jacob tried to control the part of him that might make a sarcastic response. "Then no," he said.

"You Resistance lot, always going on about us stopping you all from having kids, and you don't even care about family. I don't get it."

"Perhaps we can debate that at another time," Rommond said, "but if you really *do* care about your family, and the other families of people close to you, then you'll help us fight this common threat. For now, let's put our war on hold. Let's fight for a greater good."

"Fair enough, General," Trokus said, extending his hand. "I do this for my family."

Trokus was called away to receive a transmission from headquarters, straight from the mouth of the Iron Emperor himself. The Resistance forces were left alone at their table, where they tried not to exchange awkward looks with the Regime patrons.

"So," Jacob said, turning to Cantro. "What's your story?"

"My story?"

"Everyone's got a story. Some are better than others, but we've all got one."

"Mine isn't that exciting."

"Really? Sky pilot and all? Why'd you join the Resistance?"

Cantro sighed. "I joined this war because I lost

everything that mattered. My wife. My daughter. My grandson. You know, I don't even know if he was human. I like to think my daughter was one of the Pure. She was pure to me, and she died before she could be tainted by this world."

"Ouch," Jacob said. "Maybe I shouldn't have asked."

"Maybe you shouldn't have, but you did." He swamped down another whiskey. "And now that I'm talking, maybe I signed up because I wanted vengeance. Maybe I wanted this to never happen to another family ... even though I know it happened to many. And maybe I'm just pushing myself closer to death so that I can finally see them again."

"Heavy stuff."

"Yes. The weight of the world."

Jacob said no more. He glanced at Whistler and raised his eyebrows, and the boy returned the gesture. With all the booze and scantily-clad women, whom Whistler tried to appear like he wasn't staring at, this did not exactly seem like the family-friendly place that Trokus made out.

As Trokus took his time with that fateful phone call, Rommond pulled close to Jacob and spoke beneath his breath, keeping his mostly full drink to his mouth to disguise his words, and his eyes fixed on the dancers on the stage. He refused to sit, which made Jacob cautious to do so either.

"This could all go horribly wrong," the general reminded Jacob, as if he needed the reminder. The possibilities played out over and over in Jacob's mind, with one in particular that kept coming into view: that if the Iron Emperor refused to grant the truce, then the club was about to get a lot more crimson.

"Yeah, I kind of thought about that," Jacob said.

"I hope you're ready for a fight."

"Not really."

"Well, get ready," Rommond said, glancing around the room at all the people there—or, as he probably saw it, all the targets.

Armax shuffled up, placing a tray of drinks down on the table, and patting the general gruffly on the back. "Don't worry, Roms, we've got it covered. Bang boom, in and out, and back home for supper!"

"I'm not sure you really know what we're doing here, do you?" Jacob asked.

"Hey, it's all the same," Armax said. "Except here we can down a few before the bullets start flying. Or we start flying. Or whatever order it goes in."

"Probably safer *not* to drink before you fly," Rommond recommended.

Armax held out his hand, palm downwards, and made it tremble. "Gets rid of the shakes," he said. "Old Croc's got 'em. Surprised you don't too." He nudged Rommond. "Half me mates have shell-shock from the trenches."

"And the other half?" Jacob asked.

"They're dead."

"Ah, yes."

Rommond kept his eyes on the door to the back room that Trokus had disappeared into. "He's taking his time."

"Maybe he's got the shakes too," Jacob said.

The general watched the room like a hawk, spotting every movement, judging every gesture. When two guards strolled through and led Trokus' wife and children out, it was not a very encouraging sign. The music kept playing, and the dancers kept dancing, but the atmosphere had changed.

"Do you notice who's left?" Rommond asked his comrades.

Jacob looked around.

"Soldiers and hookers," the general continued. "In other words, the kind of people no one bats an eyelid at if they find dead."

"Oh."

"Looks like something's going down all right," Armax said, downing the last of his pint in preparation.

"So much for dialogue," Nissi said.

Whistler looked up at Jacob from his seat, sensing something.

They heard the door lock, and the lights went out.

Jacob sighed. "I guess he said *no* then."

Chapter Ten

GUNFIGHT AT CLUB CRIMSON

Jacob ducked low as he heard the sound of soldiers running into the club from the back rooms. It was pitch black inside, and he had barely gotten his bearings. He regretted not making a mental map of the room like Rommond undoubtedly had.

"Listen up," one of the soldiers roared. "Surrender now and this doesn't have to get ugly."

Rommond was silent. Jacob was not even sure if he was where he last saw him. There was not the crinkle of a coat or the cocking of a gun. Yet Jacob could not imagine the general just stood there.

Whistler! Jacob thought. Last he had seen him, he was sitting at the table, bang smack in the centre of the room, between all the potential gunfire. Jacob crawled slowly across the room towards where he thought the table was, trying to be as silent as the Desert Hawk.

"I don't hear any surrenders," the soldier said. "Slide over your guns."

Jacob slid his gun a little ahead of him to help mask the sound of his movement.

"Are you crazy?" Armax shouted. "These lads I'm with are right killers! They'll have you all for breakfast, and I'll have a bite myself, if you don't mind!"

Jacob could imagine Rommond rolling his eyes. *They don't need to see you with that mouth.* He kind of wondered how many people had said that about him too.

"This is your last warn—" The soldier grunted as a sudden gunshot cut him short.

Well, that's where Rommond is then.

The lights came on suddenly, and the glare was blinding. As Jacob squinted, he noticed the knees of a soldier just inches from his face. Jacob looked up, and the soldier looked down, and though they were enemies, they shared the same look of shock. Both had guns, a rifle versus a pistol. In the battle of seconds, the pistol always won.

As the soldier collapsed, all hell broke loose in the club. Guns rattled, glasses smashed, and tables were overturned. People ran to and fro, the soldiers shouting, the dancers screaming. In the flurry, Jacob could barely make out who was who. He tried to spot Whistler, but he was distracted by the hail of bullets flying in all directions.

He ducked behind a table, which broke into a thousand splinters as several soldiers took aim. He dived low and crawled across the floor towards the bar, where—not all that surprisingly—Armax holed up. The manic fighter popped his hands up now and then to shoot, and his head up to shout a variety of insults.

Across the other side of the room, far from where Jacob had last seen him, Rommond fired several trademark trick shots, which took out the gaslights dotted around the room. The veil drew again, but this time the Regime soldiers were the ones who trembled.

"Did you see Whistler?" Jacob whispered to Armax.

"Sorry, son," Armax said, a little too loudly. "Have you seen my lighter?"

Jacob shook his head.

Gunfire periodically illuminated the room, giving auras to silhouettes, and life to shadows. It was difficult to tell who was who, and impossible to tell what side they were on. Jacob usually liked the darkness, but that was to hide in, not fight in.

Another round of gunfire revealed a figure crouched down behind a room separator across the way. The light was not there for long, but Jacob thought he saw the outline of Whistler's messy hair. Soldiers tended to have tighter cuts than that.

Jacob darted out, crawling across the room between each brief flash of ignited gunpowder, keeping as low as possible, and trying his best to scramble behind something solid before the light betrayed him. He had spent too long in the shadows for the light to do anything else.

He paused near the staircase, bumping into Nissi, who raised her eyebrows at him, as if she was enjoying the show. She did not speak, but her face said enough: *Now this is entertainment.* It was little surprise that she and Armax volunteered on this mission. Jacob just wondered why he was also one of them.

Eventually he made it over to Whistler, startling the boy when he grabbed his arm. Whistler had his hands over his ears, and his eyes were squinted shut.

Half his cover was blown apart by bullets, and there were holes in the wall nearby. No one in the room left standing could really attribute that to luck; it was just that the furniture had a lot less of it than them.

Jacob ushered Whistler out into the open after another round of gunfire. Whistler was not as good at being quiet as Jacob was, which resulted in a few bullets fired their way. Eventually they made it back to the bunker of the bar, where Armax had lined up a series of half-full whiskey bottles, stuffed with old handkerchiefs. He grinned at them and flicked on his rediscovered lighter.

"Hell," Jacob said.

"Sorry, did you want to do the honour?" Armax asked him.

"Eh, no."

The gunfire continued in the darkness for a moment, then died down as everyone checked to see if the other side was dead. One of the Regime soldiers lit a gas lamp on the wall, and Jacob saw Rommond standing behind the soldiers near the back door. They barely had time to express shock before he shot them all and quickly reloaded.

"Damn!" Armax said, holding up the lit bottle. "What am I to do with this then?"

"Leave it," Rommond replied.

Armax dropped the bottle, and the flames engulfed the bar, growing as they encountered more bottles and kegs. Armax snuck away, as if he had nothing to do with it. Jacob and Whistler swiftly followed.

They hurried out the back door, and halted when

they found Trokus alone there.

"Quick!" he said. "Follow me."

Rommond aimed his gun. "I'd rather not."

"Look, the Iron Emperor gave his orders," Trokus said. "I'm defying them. If you want to get those planes we have, then follow me. I know the fastest route."

There was little time to debate, and no time to gain trust. Necessity urged them on, and Rommond reluctantly holstered his weapon.

They followed Trokus through a series of rooms and corridors, and down into a dimly-lit basement, which led to a series of tunnels beneath the town. Trokus stopped suddenly at the end of the last tunnel, with one foot on the ladder leading up into a storehouse.

"When we enter here," he said, "we won't have long before guards across Rustport are alerted. They'll start shutting down the aerodrome and runway immediately. Even your Landquaker won't be much use then. I've sent men loyal to me to cause a distraction, but we'll only have a few minutes to get from this storehouse to the main hanger, and we'll have a hard time getting there unseen."

"Why are you helping us?" Jacob asked.

"I'm not doing this for you. I'm doing this for my family. It's like Rommond says. None of this war will matter if that bomb goes off."

Armax placed his hand on Trokus' shoulder. "I might have burnt down your club."

Trokus did not know what to say, and Armax did not stay around to hear it. He joined Rommond and the others as they clambered up the ladder. The storehouse was full of giant crates and barrels, the kind they had seen hauled by even larger cranes at the docks.

They opened the door and looked outside. There was no one there, but it was a long stretch of land between them and the hanger, and it was broad daylight. It would be easy to spot them racing across. Everything depended on speed, and Trokus' loyal supporters.

Let's hope it's some distraction, Jacob thought.

"You can't get us any closer?" Rommond asked the commander.

"This is as close as the tunnels get. Everything else is overground."

"Well, I guess we make a run for it then," Jacob said.

They looked again at their destination, and prepared to make the sprint.

A sudden alarm rang out, long and droning.

"Damn it, we've been outed!" Armax cried.

"That's not an intruder alarm," Rommond said.

"No," Trokus said. "That's an air raid siren."

Chapter Eleven

PAPER ORDNANCE

"We don't have time for this!" Rommond growled. "We'll have to make a dash for it."

"With bombs falling?" Jacob asked.

"Then we better run quick."

The general charged out, and after a moment of hesitation the others followed. All round, the bomb sirens blared, rising and falling, and setting all minds on edge.

They raced across the open ground, keenly aware that they stood out like targets to the bombers above. They had to hope that speed would save them. They had to hope the bombs would not fall along their path.

Further afield, soldiers dived into bunkers, and sailors cast out in dinghies on the docks, leaving behind their larger ships, which were most likely to be hit. There was a clamour of screams and shouts, competing with the clangour of the alarm.

Any who dared look up saw the hot air balloons floating overhead, unloading their payload, which from this vantage point looked like little black specks, before spreading into a multitude of black specks that seemed to span the entire sky.

"Cluster bombs!" Nissi shouted.

Rommond ran faster, and his frenzy spurred them all on. He knew war better than all of them combined. He knew when to fight, and when to hide—and when to run as if fear itself lashed at his heels.

Jacob kept his eyes on the hangar across the way. No matter how fast he fled, it still seemed very far away. And then, to his horror, the hangar doors started to close slowly. The soldiers inside must have spotted them. Or if they were loyal to Trokus, they were loyal to their own lives first, and tried to seal themselves inside from the blast.

As the arsenal of the air came ever closer, and they raced faster, and the doors ahead seemed to taunt them, Jacob glanced back and noticed that Whistler was falling behind. Without a hint of hesitation, despite the imminence of death, the smuggler slowed and stopped, and ran back towards the boy, pulling and ushering him on.

Then they heard a sharp whistle, which almost rent their ears, and they were startled by the sudden crash of a metal bomb casing less than a metre to their left. It cracked the ground, but to their surprise and gratitude, it did not explode.

They charged forward, painfully aware of the gap between them and the others as much as the gap between them and the closing hangar doors. Jacob dared not look, but he could see the impending shapes in his peripheral vision, the dark blotches coming into view, coming into land.

He saw Rommond approaching the hangar door,

and reaching for his pistol. A guard inside threw himself to the floor, but that's where the general sent the bullet. Another fled, and the door was left ajar, just in time for some of them to race inside.

But Rommond halted, stopping out in the open, just inches from the safety of the hangar. He looked up, shaking his head, as if it was all futile, as if there were no bunkers strong enough to withstand what came for them—as if it were the Worldwaker itself.

Yet what came down upon them did not rock the bunkers or pierce the roofs. It did not topple walls or take lives. The balloon bombers dropped no explosives. They sent down leaflet bombs, shells containing paper instead of gunpowder. They opened mid-air, releasing their ink-filled ordnance, which fell down gently, a light rain instead of hail, the wind catching them and cradling them, and sending them down like parachutes.

Jacob shielded his face from the flutter of the flyers, and when he and Whistler caught up with the general, he saw him clutching one of the pamphlets, on the cover of which read in bold writing: *WAKE UP!* Rommond rolled his eyes as he flicked through the booklet, with its stark warnings and exaggerated images, telling the people that they were sleeping, that they must join "the cause of the waking," and rise up against those would keep them in slumber. The problem was that the Armageddon Brigade planned to achieve their aim by murder and suicide. *Life is a dream*, they claimed. *A bad dream they make you keep on dreaming.*

"I suppose it's not so bad," Armax said, holding

up one of the leaflets.

"It's worse," the general replied. "We can't have people believing this nonsense. It endangers everything."

"But it's just paper—"

"Just words," Rommond said. "People die for words, for concepts, for ideas. We've been dying for ours. There's a reason the Iron Emperor outlawed literature. It educates. It inspires. Those are dangerous things. And the problem is, in the absence of real information, it is nonsense like this that people start believing in. And *that* is even more dangerous." He slapped the pamphlet into Armax's chest.

"Look at this one," Armax said, snatching a leaflet from the wind. He held it up to Rommond, where it showed the general's own likeness, albeit with horns, red eyes, and a halo of fire. The caption read: *HIS TRUE FORM.*

"They can't be serious," Rommond said.

Jacob could not help but notice a glimmer of smugness on Trokus' face. *Your turn to be demonised*, he imagined him thinking.

"Kind of hard to believe they're serious about any of this," Jacob said.

"They really think I'm a demon."

"Says here," Armax added, reading from the back, "that you orchestrated this whole thing, that you're the Dreamkeeper."

"No," Rommond said, scrunching the leaflet up into a tiny ball. "I'm the Dreamdestroyer."

Chapter Twelve

FLIGHT

They entered the hanger, which had been partly evacuated due to the air raid, and the rest from Rommond's gunfire. The handful of soldiers who remained were those loyal to Trokus, and with them was the commander's son, Markus. His wife and daughter were not there to wish him a safe journey. There were no safe journeys to be had.

"Right," Armax said, clapping his hands together loudly, "which wingship's mine?"

Rommond did not bother asking. He charged over to one of the monoplanes, inspected its number, grimaced at the sight of the Regime emblem on the side, and then hopped inside. By the time the others chose their aircraft, or were assigned them, the general was already firing his up.

"Mind if I take this one?" Whistler asked, just as Jacob was about to climb into one of the few remaining monoplanes. Everyone was in a hurry to get one of the newer models, even though they all knew very little about them.

"Sure, but why?" Jacob said.

"The number." Whistler pointed to the tail fin, which had the number fourteen painted on it in large red letters.

"Pity there's no thirty-six."

Whistler gestured to the last remaining aircraft, a rather rusty-looking biplane, which looked less like one of Brooklyn's designs and more like one of his ancestors. It bore the number eleven, chipped and faded, on its hull.

"You can be a kid again," Whistler said with a smile.

Jacob climbed up to the cockpit of his biplane, cringing at the sound of the metal and wood creaking from his weight. Every noise was like the voice of his doubt and regret.

Well, he thought, *you did volunteer*.

He sat down in the leather seat, feeling around for the seat belt. There were a lot of them, which was not reassuring. He supposed it was better than falling out. A pair of dust-covered goggles stared at him from the dashboard.

He jumped when the radio clicked on. He heard Trokus' voice crackle through.

"This is a secure channel. Only open to us."

"Good," Rommond replied.

"A few things before we take off," Trokus said. "You'll notice a lever beneath your seat."

"Pull it?" Armax asked.

"No! Don't pull it!"

"I'm just messing with you."

Trokus was clearly not amused. "That's the ejection mechanism. If you pull that, it will dislodge the pilot seat, and pressurised cylinders will fire it up into the air, before triggering a parachute sixty seconds later."

"Well, that's good to have," Jacob said.

"The problem," Trokus continued, "is that it'll break your back in the process, but at least it's better than dying."

"Less keen on it now."

"What about a more conventional exit?" Rommond asked. "A standard parachute."

"You should have one of those as well, near your feet."

"I don't," the general said.

"Right. We'll get you one now. In the meantime, our pilots will quickly go over the controls."

The Regime's crash course was very basic, just enough to stop them from plotting a crash course of their own.

"What are all these?" Jacob asked, gesturing to numerous dials on the dashboard.

"Don't worry about them," Trokus said.

"Just for show?"

"No, but best to keep things simple."

I just hope they're not what I need for landing, Jacob thought.

"You all set?" Trokus asked him, checking that he had a parachute.

"Not really, but it's too late to back out now, right?"

Trokus forced a smile and slammed the canopy down.

* * *

Trokus returned to his own vessel, a much larger biplane with room for a separate gunner as well as a pilot. From the looks of it, there was space for a few more as well. He was the first to leave the hangar and take flight, followed by Rommond and Cantro. Then it was Jacob's turn.

Jacob turned on the engine and fed the furnace behind him. He could already feel the heat building inside. Steam funnelled out of a small chimney towards the rear of the vessel. For every exhalation from the aircraft, Jacob had an apprehensive one of his own.

"Good luck," Whistler spoke through the radio. Jacob saw the kid giving a thumbs up from his own plane. "I'm sure you won't need it," he added.

"I don't know about that," Jacob replied.

The smuggler pushed on the accelerator, and the vessel rolled forward towards the now open hangar doors.

"Use the full length of the runway," Trokus said. "Don't try to take off too early."

Not sure I want to take off at all, Jacob thought. He wondered if taxiing around the runway throughout the battle counted as sufficient contribution to the war effort. *Probably not.*

He drove onto the runway, slow at first, then started to pick up speed. It was a long stretch, and he had to fight the urge to pull up early. He felt the wind waft beneath the wings, and the rocking of the vessel beneath him on the stone path.

Rommond's voice came over the radio. "There's an old saying for times like this. Fear is leaden.

Courage is golden. Let go of the weight of the world, and you will fly."

The end of the runway approached, and though Jacob had prepared for it, it seemed to come quicker than he expected. He had to pull up soon or he would career off the road into the dunes that lined the aerodrome like a wall.

"Keep it steady," Cantro urged, but it was anything but steady.

The moment came, and Jacob pulled back on the steering stick. He felt the nose of the plane rise, and the wind swept beneath him. The rocking of the road changed to a gentle glide as he ascended into the sky.

He heard Whistler cheering through the radio, and glanced back to see that the boy was already taxiing up to the runway. Everyone still grounded seemed eager to get airborne, but now that Jacob was in the air, the mission came clearly into view, and it was a daunting one.

"So," Jacob spoke into the radio, "not to sound pessimistic or anything, but even if we do catch up, how do we get on board?"

"Simple," Rommond replied. "We jump."

"And … that's what I was afraid you were going to say."

"You have your parachute, but you shouldn't engage it unless you miss the mark."

"That's … also what I'm afraid of."

"We need the aid of gravity on this one. We'll fly overhead, and jump onto the hull. From there we'll make our way on board."

"Easy peasy," Armax said, rocking the wings of

his monoplane from side to side. "Just don't look down!" he added with a manic laugh.

Chapter Thirteen

THE DUNE BURROWS

Alex led Brooklyn to and through the great mountainous range of sand known as the Dune Burrows, colossal bodies of dust that rose and fell, and rose again, forming towering heights and tremendous drops. Yet these were not merely the work of nature, which nursed them in their youth, for man and maran came and dug deep into the dunes, hollowing them out for homes, raiding them for the treasures of the earth. They were now abandoned, the temporary refuge of only archaeologists.

"Aren't they b-b-beautiful?" Alex said, basking in the monstrous sight.

Brooklyn could see an element of beauty, but also an element of ugliness. They were misshapen. The natural formations had been scarred and abused by people, and left only when there was nothing left to extract. So much of Altadas was like that now. As the days passed, it resembled more and more the husk of the demon home world.

"These were the worship places of the old g-gods," Alex revealed. "There are burial chambers in many of them, and temples with sand altars that still stand today. Of course, t-t-tomb robbers have been through

91

these thoroughly, so there is little of 'value' left—and yet, to the archaeologist and the historian, a lot can still be found."

It was not long before they found what might at first have seemed like relics of the past, but were newly-carved statues of the Iron Emperor, deliberately aged to make it seem like he had always been there, that the ancients did not worship some other pantheon. They worshipped him.

"Aren't they fascinating?" Alex asked.

If anything, Brooklyn found them revolting. Though they were etched to show off the Iron Emperor's supposed beauty—just as his visage on the coils were—time sculpted them anew, as it did to all living, and all lifeless. The face was hideous now, like maybe it really was to those not under his spell.

Further afield there were the stunted ruins of other Regime statues, with only the feet and ankles remaining. Time was not to blame for those. The broken remains lay nearby from the blast of a bomb.

They travelled through the canyons, between the steepest of dunes, and up the less precipitous ones, until they came to a wall of sand, through which was a mighty gate of iron, up to which was a colossal set of stairs.

"They built big," Brooklyn noted.

"Well, the gods were big then."

"And now?"

"Now there's only one god worth noting, and he's the size of a maran."

"The Iron Emperor."

They began their climb, already weary, and the

sun tried to steal whatever strength they had left. It was another god, a forgotten god, who gave a daily reminder, and was forgotten again each night. The new religious sect that started in Blackout tried to revive those ancient mysteries, but the people of Altadas had grown weary as well, and now only trusted in iron.

They hiked across the dunes, barely stopping to rest. Alex went into great detail about the types of rock and sand, and periodically halted to inspect something, and sometimes sprinted forward, brush in hand, to unearth the world's next greatest treasure. Most of these moments were fruitless, while the others resulted in shards of pottery and scraps of parchment, the kind of things that made an archaeologist giddy, but meant little to everybody else.

The journey was not uneventful for Brooklyn, however. When halfway through the Burrows, the ground rocked, and the sky darkened suddenly. Lightning extended from a central point in the heavens, which grew suddenly like a window into another world. It was very far up, so it was difficult to see what that world was like, but it coughed out noxious fumes, and a thick red dust blew through, adding to the dunes.

"What's that?" Brooklyn shouted as the earth continued to quake.

"That's the Rift."

"Here?" Brooklyn asked. "I thought it opened further east."

"It travels," Alex explained. "Almost g-got a life of its own." He shuddered at the notion.

"It is pity we cannot close it for good."

"Or k-k-keep it open, and send the demons back." He paused for a moment, shielding his eyes as he stared up at the portal. "You know, I wouldn't mind an expedition through there some time. I'm sure it's a f-fascinating place. Just imagine the digs!"

"I'd rather not think about world of monsters," Brooklyn said.

Alex laughed. "*This* is the world of monsters now."

Chapter Fourteen

COMMSPIRE OASIS

The task of finding and freeing Doctor Mudro was significant, and the Resistance's resources were slim. Brute force would not work in this scenario. Taberah was sure of that. They needed a different kind of approach.

"A distraction," Taberah suggested. "Just what Mudro would have done."

"Why doesn't he do it then?" Gregan sneered.

Taberah rolled her eyes at him. "He's a little preoccupied."

"What do you propose?" Leadman asked.

"We wave one hand, then free him with the other."

"Sounds nice on paper, but what's the hand we wave?"

"I don't know that yet," Taberah admitted.

"If only I had my equipment," Tardo said with a sigh.

"Your equipment?"

"My comms gear. Anything I had was destroyed by Jacob. I could have used it to distract them. They don't yet know I've defected."

"Maybe we can salvage some equipment from

the Landquaker."

Tardo shook his head. "I already looked. There's little there that isn't damaged. The good radios were taken by the fleeing troops."

"Then what are we waiting for?" Leadman barked. "Let's go chase them."

"They're long gone by now," Tardo said. "And the Iron Emperor probably had them killed for deserting the field of battle. You fight and die, or you die. Dying is the common element."

"Where's the nearest Commspire?" Taberah asked.

Tardo mouthed silently as he thought to himself. "I think that's Commspire Oasis."

"Oasis," Leadman mused. "That's not that far at all."

"They're pretty heavily armed," Tardo said.

"So are we," Taberah replied. "We can storm them."

Leadman shook his head. "I have a better plan."

They travelled without pause, and it was not long before the Commspire came into view. It was a thin iron tower, from which a gigantic aerial extended, part of the Regime's vast communications network, and one of the toys Rommond greatly coveted, yet found difficult to implement successfully. At the base of the tower was a large hexagonal bunker, with big anti-tank guns pointing out from watch posts at all six corners, and similar anti-aircraft guns pointing up to the sky, giving it significant protection from all angles.

"Are you sure this will work?" Taberah asked Leadman.

"No," he replied, "but it's better than your plan of all guns blazing."

Gregan nodded. "Especially when they've got bigger guns."

The guards patrolled around the top of the Commspire tower, strolling and chatting, their rifles ready. Inside the hexagonal base of the tower, the gunner guards kept their own watch, adjusting their guns every so often, targeting tumbleweed and desert scorpions.

"Did you hear he's going to be there?" one of the guards said to his comrade, who lounged back, arms behind his head.

"Yeah, I've got family going," the other guard replied.

"Should be quite a speech. Too bad I'm on duty."

The guard looked out again, and for a moment he thought he saw something. He strained his eyes, but all he saw was a wall of sand in that direction. He had grown so used to the dunes that he almost yearned to see something else.

"I'd bet you a whole coil that he's going to announce something big," the second guard said. "He did at the last rally. I bet we caught the Scorpion or something."

The first guard kept his eye fixed on the terrain ahead. The sand shifted a little. He thought they were probably in for a sandstorm.

"Wasn't Rommond captured recently too?" he

asked, turning back to his comrade.

"I heard that as well."

The first guard looked out again. The sand seemed closer now than ever. The dunes were always shifting. It was likely a cartographer's nightmare. The way the sands were moving now, it seemed like the storm was coming fast.

The dust-covered bulldozer landship kept its steady advance, pushing the sand ahead of it, disguising its snail-like movement towards the Commspire. Leadman worked out the perfect angle of attack, where they were in the blind spot of two guns, and could only be seen head-on from the third. Yet, any slight divergence could give them up, and they did not have the benefit of being able to see where they were going. They had to take their time, yet every second sought to oust them.

"You won't have long to get inside," Leadman told Taberah. "We need those anti-landship guns disabled quick."

"I'll be quick," she said.

"And you," Leadman said, turning to Tardo, "you better get control of the aerial ASAP, or we'll have half the Regime looking for us, and the Hold will be on high alert."

Tardo gulped at the notion. "I'll try."

"You better do more than try," the general berated, "or we all die."

Inside the guard post, the first guard felt increasingly like there was something wrong with his vision, or something off about the terrain. The dune crept closer towards his position, but it did not look that windy out, and the other hills stayed still.

"Does something about that look funny to you?" he asked his comrade.

The second guard groaned and came over. "It's always the same with you," he complained. "I told you this was a cushy number. Communications aren't on the front line. We're more likely to die of thirst out here than anything else." He glanced inside the eyeglass. "So? What am I looking for?"

"There," the first guard said, pointing down, almost to the wall of the tower itself.

"What? It's sand."

"I know it's sand, but that was back there a minute ago."

"Sand moves, you know."

"Ugh, you never take me seriously!"

"Wait," the second guard said. "What's that?"

They both looked, and had to check again. Something was coming out of the sand dune. At first they thought it was a snake or scorpion, but they were wrong. It was a turret.

The guard post exploded in a ball of flame, and neither guard had to worry about looking outside again.

Taberah and Gregan raced through the chasm blown by the landship, splitting up immediately as they made for the remaining two guard posts on that side of the Commspire. There were few guards inside, as no one expected the enemy to get that close, and they were no match for the experience and firepower of the Resistance.

Taberah reached her target and immediately set about placing explosives around the sealed door. While she worked, a solitary soldier turned the corner, halted in surprise, then fell dead to her pistol.

The door exploded, and Taberah killed both guards inside. They were ready at their anti-landship gun, but it pointed in the wrong direction. They did not expect the Scorpion's sting from behind.

She rejoined Gregan just as Tardo rushed inside with his toolbox. "Up the Revolution!" he cheered, raising a spanner.

"Not really the time," Taberah said. That youthful enthusiasm for the Resistance was killed off quick in new recruits, if they were not killed off first.

They headed up to the next level, killing as they went, until they breached the control room for the aerial itself. The mechanics inside were kept alive, at gunpoint, while Tardo got to work taking over the broadcast.

"Right," he said. "I'm all set here. I can create a private channel just for us. Or I can send targeted broadcasts. Or pretty much anything you want."

"Can you end the war?" Gregan replied.

Tardo shrugged.

"Prepare a broadcast for the Hold," Taberah ordered.

"Security's tight there. It'll take a while."

"Then you better get started."

As Taberah moved to leave the room, Gregan pulled her aside.

"Do you trust him?" he asked. "He is one of *them*, after all."

"More than I trust you," she replied. "You're one of Leadman's men, after all."

He bared his teeth at her, as if it was mandatory for the Crocodile's men to show their bite.

"Where are you off to, anyway?" he asked.

"To free another Magus from his cell."

Chapter Fifteen

CACTUS X

Taberah took the Silver Ghost alone out into the wild, watching carefully to see if she was being followed, by either Regime *or* Resistance forces. This was a mission for the Order, and there were few members left. She was not entirely sure if any would be left standing when the war was over.

She left the sands behind and passed the un-marked barrier into the unwatched lands of the Wild North, keeping as close to the edge as possible, away from the heartland where the criminals congregated. The earth was cracked and broken, and the only flora around were a variety of widely-spaced cacti, and the only fauna around was a certain ruby-haired Scorpion.

She halted the Silver Ghost and stepped outside, again looking to and fro to see if anyone had spotted her. This had become routine for her in this part of the Wild North, a kind like any other to most people, but as distinctive as a landmark to her.

She circled one of the larger, solitary cacti. It was twice her height, and several times her width, with many prickly spines pointing out in all directions from its bulbous hide. There were plenty like it in the area, big and small, and varying in shape, but this was the only one with faint footsteps nearby.

Taberah gave another routine glance. Only the desert's eyes looked back.

"Gouet," she said. There was a tiny tremor in the cactus.

Taberah waited for a moment, but nothing else happened. "Gouet!" she said again, this time much louder.

Suddenly, small metal legs emerged from the base of the cactus, and it hauled up and crept several feet away.

Taberah followed it, then kicked at part of it that was not shielded with thorns. Part of the flesh of the cactus shifted, and from the square opening that formed there emerged an eyeglass.

"It's me," Taberah said, as the eyeglass looked her up and down.

Even more suddenly, the cactus cracked in half like an egg, opening out to reveal an inner metal sphere, lined on either side with laboratory equipment. Sitting on a rotating stool in the centre was a man of great years, hunched over, with long, thin strands of white hair, and a mangy beard to match.

"I haven't heard from you in a long time," the man said weakly, holding out a shaking hand.

"I know," Taberah said. "I've been busy."

"Too busy for this?" he asked, gesturing to hundreds of amulets lining the walls of his oddball dwelling. "I've been waiting for a collection. What happened to your smugglers?"

"They got busy too," she replied. "Most with the

afterlife."

"I can't help them with that. Only the start of life."

"I need your help with something else, Gouet."

"I'm not good for much here," Gouet said. "I'm not good for long either." He ran the bony fingers of his left hand across the many wrinkles on his face.

"Then we have to hurry."

"What about these?" he asked, pointing to the amulets once again.

"They're just treating the symptoms," Taberah said. "We're going to find the cure."

Chapter Sixteen

WAR OF THE WEATHER

Most of the fifteen working aircraft took flight without a hitch, with only one forced to land due to a faulty engine. Several others remained grounded for repairs, or because they were deemed too unsafe to fly. Jacob thought that should probably have applied to all of them, and his creaking craft most of all.

As they gained height, they spotted the balloon bombers floating away in all directions, and realised that they had been unmanned. They were unlike the vibrant vessels of the Treasury, trading bright colours for sombre greys. It seemed that they had saved their pigments for the flashy cartoons in their leaflets, and for the gaudy yellow of the Dreamdevil itself.

Armax shot down one the wandering balloons, cheering loudly over the radio at his success.

"Save those bullets," Rommond cautioned. "We may yet meet some who shoot back."

The weather had been kind for take-off, for which the novice pilots were more than grateful, but the skies further north were not as pleasant as those over Rustport. Black clouds loomed ahead, the Iron Wall of the sky. Darkness gathered there, smothering out the sunlight. As the fleet headed towards it, it threatened to smother them too.

"Maybe we should go around," Whistler suggested.

"We don't have time for that," Rommond said. "We're already way behind."

"What about under?" the boy proposed.

Jacob glanced down. It was hard to see much below from that vantage point, but it was clear that the dark clouds were there too. It almost seemed like they reached straight down to the ground itself, like the wafting smog of a monumental bomb.

"I think we're stuck here," Jacob said.

"We go through or we give up," Rommond replied. No one took that as a choice.

"I guess we go through then. I hope you've got better eyesight than I do." The goggles helped with the glare of the sun, but they also dulled his vision. The clouds did a lot of that as well.

"There's that old eagle eye of the Hawk," Armax said with great enthusiasm.

Rommond was less encouraging. "Tonight we're all bats. We're flying blind."

"At least bats can fly," Jacob commented. He had gained precious little confidence in the flying power of Brooklyn's machines. They might have been the engineer's designs, and those were not so bad, but they were finished by the Regime's engineers, and those were much worse.

They dived into the ocean of shadow and smog, adding to it with the fumes of their own aircraft. The goggles were useless now, but Jacob kept them on, in case there might be some break in the murky pool. It was fitting that the Worldwaker had passed through there, with the shark emblem painted on brightly. In those deep waters, it could not be seen. It almost felt like it had lured them in. The dolphins do not hunt the sharks.

"I'm not seeing anything," Jacob said, trying to control the quiver in his voice as much as the gear sticks. It was difficult to tell where anything was, both the wings of his own plane and the wings of the others. It was impossible to tell what direction was up. It was more important to know what direction was down.

"Join the club," Armax replied.

"Kind of want to leave it," the smuggler retorted.

"Isn't it cool?" Whistler said, with not a hint of hesitation. "We could be anywhere."

"Yeah," Jacob said derisively, "like heading towards the ground."

Static greeted him over the radio as the fliers focused on the flight. It only added to Jacob's anxiety, like the suffocating silence of the ocean depths.

"You're awfully quiet there, Rommond."

"I'm concentrating," the general drawled.

Nissi's voice crackled through. "Think we all should be."

"Indeed."

Jacob was not so sure. "I think I need to talk."

"Evidently."

"You still there, Whistler?" Jacob asked.

"Yeah, I'm here." He sounded a lot closer, which was less comforting. It was not just *too close for comfort* in the skies; it was *too close for living*. He could almost feel the wings tipping each other, and hoped it was just his imagination. The heat was getting to him, but he could not blame his perspiration on the temperature alone.

They sailed through, but it was not entirely silent in the abyss of the sky. Just like the submarine that Jacob never wanted to return to, his new vessel groaned from the pressure of the air. He could hear the bolts straining, and he could feel the wood and steel quiver beneath his own quivering feet.

Then a new sound came.

It seemed like a low growl, as if there was a creature inside the clouds. It rumbled again, as if they had disturbed its nest. Once more it came, closer and louder, and from everywhere at once, as if they had strayed into the belly of a slumbering beast.

Then everything turned brilliant white for a second, and Jacob's eyes were stunned. The shock faded, but then another flash came, dulled by the darkness of the fog. Blades of lightning broke through the sea of smoke, accompanied by the violent clap of thunder, as if an angry god saw the storm devour them, and burst out into wild applause.

Jacob narrowly missed a lashing bolt. They struck so fast that it was virtually impossible to dodge them. They had to be predicted instead. There was a certain sizzle in the air, a kind of build up, like something was about to happen. Maybe it was just a hidden hint of science, or maybe it was something spiritual. Jacob did not care. He only cared that it helped save his life.

As the planes dashed and dodged, and the electric

fingers reached out ever closer to them, the wind joined the fray, and then the rain, and it all stirred together in the cauldron of the storm. The wings and propellers were just another ingredient.

The sky rumbled in anger. The lightning crushed like teeth, and the black clouds tried to swallow them. What could not be eaten only seemed to upset the rolling, toiling monster of the air even more. As they battled against the winds and the rain, and fought with the controls of their own vessels, many of the pilots saw why the people of bygone times looked up to nature's marvels in the heavens and gave them the names of gods.

They pulled through the last of the dark clouds, and were blinded by the sun ahead. They regained control of their aircraft, and breathed a much-needed sigh of relief, though not all came out to breathe it. Two of Trokus' men were lost in the haze. It was unclear if they had plummeted to the ground or were simply swallowed whole by the billowing dragon.

Jacob tore off his steamed-up goggles, rubbed the sweat from his fringe, and cast an anxious glance around until he saw the number fourteen brightly emblazoned on one of the monoplanes ahead.

He was tempted to make some remark about their luck, but fought successfully against the urge. *We're far too close to the fates right now*, he thought.

The relief of the pilots must have been audible, because Rommond's foreboding voice crackled through on the radio. "Don't rest easy just yet." They could not see him, but his tone almost pointed straight ahead. There, in the distance, unobscured by cloud and unhindered by hail, were a fleet of planes bearing the explosive emblem of the Armageddon Brigade.

The attack of the weather was over, but the onslaught of iron and steel was about to begin.

Chapter Seventeen

THE BLACK FIELDS

A lex led Brooklyn out of the Dune Burrows and into the barren flatlands of Regime territory. There they found themselves faced with a large, seemingly endless, expanse of blackened sand and soil, through which a few solitary gnarled branches reached up, like the hands of the dead. It was a desolate place, more barren than even the red and yellow sands that smothered much of Altadas.

"They call these the B-b-black Fields," Alex said.

"I see why," Brooklyn replied.

Then he caught a glimpse of a small figure in the distance, as black as the land around it.

"There's someone out there," Brooklyn said.

"There are many out there," Alex corrected, pointing here and there to figures dotted periodically in the distance, whom at first could have been mistaken for those same gnarled branches. "This is where they come to d-die," Alex explained.

Brooklyn looked at him, surprised.

"They are the Hopeless, the outcasts of the maran people. They committed some crime against the Iron Emperor. Who knows what? Maybe they did not do what they were t-t-told. Maybe they expressed an opinion. Maybe they suggested ending this war. Whatever their crime, they were denied the life-sustaining Hope as punishment, and left out here to rot and roam, until they w-wither away and become new black sand."

As Alex spoke, Brooklyn could see the sick marans stumbling to and fro, some collapsing, some struggling to get back up. Others simply stood there, while many of them crumbled apart, some losing entire limbs, others dissolving into dust one little speck at a time.

Brooklyn could not hide his horror. "This land … is people?"

"Not so different than burying our own dead, if you ask me."

"There are black sands in Uga Ludomu," Brooklyn said. "They were blackened by Regime. We thought they used fire. Now … I'm not sure."

"The Regime committed many atrocities when they came here," Alex said, "and still do. It's how they k-k-keep us in check, and their own people in check. You should see what they did to some of the old archaeological sites. Desecration! But then our people do it too. You saw the stunts of statues in the Dune Burrows. The Resistance blew those up. But they're part of our history, our heritage, now. They *are* monsters, but we're monsters too. In some ways, we d-deserve each other."

That idea did not sit well with Brooklyn. He was as much a pacifist as Alex was, and yet he made tools of war, the kinds of machines that could—and probably did—blow up those statues. He knew why they were destroyed. They were not history, because the war was still happening. They were symbols. While they stood, the Iron Emperor stood. So the hope was that felling them might, like some kind of sympathetic magic, result in the Regime's leader falling too.

"Duck!" Alex cried suddenly.

Brooklyn hid in the brush, where he could hear the sound of an approaching steamtruck. It passed by swiftly, circling around the field. A soldier in the back prepped a rifle, before shooting one of the wandering Hopeless in the head.

"Almost a m-m-mercy," Alex whispered, but it did not look merciful.

The truck continued on, zig-zagging through the black crops, taking out any of the stumbling marans, who collapsed and crumbled to the ground, making it a little blacker than before. The hum of its engine faded away, leaving behind a deathly silence, which even the wind dared not disturb.

"Onwards!" Alex said, seemingly unfazed by the grim graveyard he then strolled through. That he worked digging up the dead was perhaps an aid, a kind of protective sarcophagus for the heart, but Brooklyn found it difficult to conceive how anyone could not be moved to action at the sight of the Black Fields.

"If I was not in Resistance," he said, "I would be now."

"Well," Alex replied. "You just w-w-wait till you see the Iron Emperor."

Chapter Eighteen

CONFLICT IN THE CLOUDS

"Incoming," Trokus said.

They did not need the announcement. Even in their glass bubbles, they could hear the hum of the engines, and see the streams of smoke left behind as the Armageddon Brigade's fighter planes approached. All of them were black, which contrasted starkly with both the luminous yellow of the Dreamdevil, and the more earthy tones of the Regime's fleet. The yellow mushroom cloud emblazoned on the sides of those vessels stood out brightly. It was unsurprising that they had the word Nightmare stencilled beneath.

"Evasive tactics," Rommond called out. "In three … two … one."

Right on time, a hail of bullets came, and Rommond pulled sharply to the right. Jacob turned left, and the rest of the fleet spread apart in different directions, crossing over each other haphazardly. Everywhere Jacob wanted to go, there was someone else. He could hear the rattle of gunfire off the hull, and hoped he would not feel the patter of that same gunfire on his body.

He saw Whistler's plane spinning wildly, and thought for a moment he had been hit, until he saw it dive and duck, and somersault across the clouds with ease. Jacob could barely fly in a straight line, and was not confident enough that the clouds would let him attempt any acrobatics.

That the enemy fighters were clearly marked was a blessing, but Jacob found it difficult to aim while he was struggling to get out of the aim of others. It was not just the hail of the enemy he had to worry about, but the flying bullets of his comrades, criss-crossing over each other like their own planes.

Jacob rattled off a series of short spurts of gunfire, careful not to add more metal to the mayhem than was needed. Yet his conservatism with the trigger did not help his kill count, which stayed at zero, nor did it help much with the aerial battlefield, for the others made up for his reluctance with liberal sheets of iron rain.

Trokus and his men were not naturals like Whistler, but they were highly trained. The commander used a variety of codewords over the radio, which not even Rommond knew, and then broke apart in time, or flew in formation, or focused fire, until it seemed like they were all fingers of the same hand.

Elsewhere, Armax fired madly, Nissi played bait, and trigger-shy Whistler did not fire a single bullet. Rommond alone of the Resistance seemed to own the sky. He dove low, and came up at the Armageddon Brigade from beneath, firing in short, sharp spasms when he was just metres from crashing into them. It took a while for Jacob to figure out why the general chose this tactic. For him, it was not conservation; it was skill. From the bottom, the enemy's planes were a larger target. From up close, they were larger still.

The Desert Hawk earned his name in the sky that day, and undoubtedly benefited as much from Brooklyn's know-how as he did from his own. Time and time again he used the same dive and rise to bring about the permanent dive of a Nightmare. Even when the enemy pilots learned his manoeuvre, he faked a retreat, or led them on a wild goose chase while Trokus and the others copied his tactic from above.

Planes tumbled from the heavens left and right, leaving behind a slowly fading pillar of smoke. They heard the screams of one of Trokus' men over the radio as he veered towards the ground. Then they heard Cantro's muted cry as his bullet-riddled plane started to dive. It did not matter which side they were on. They all fell the same.

Jacob found success in staying alive, and hoped that would pay off later in the end, but every dodge seemed closer than the last, and though the Nightmares were fading quickly from the sky, it seemed like those that remained were focusing on the aircraft they deemed easier prey. Like him.

There were six Brigade vessels left, and four of them hunted Jacob, forcing him to break away from the others as he desperately tried to dodge the concentrated gunfire aimed his way. As he veered from the herd, and out of radio contact, he realised his error, but realised it too late.

Two of the Nightmares disappeared into the clouds, while the other two stayed on him from behind. There was some relief in seeing half the enemy vanish, but much dread in wondering where they had gone. He zig-zagged across the heavens, from side to side, and up and down, and every direction he could think of, and every angle his instincts bade him go.

Then the two other aircraft reappeared ahead, facing him diagonally. They fired, creating an intersecting lane of shrapnel straight ahead, which they pushed towards him. The two fighters at the rear copied this approach, until all four had boxed him in, unable to go anywhere but up or down. He tried up, but they reacted quick, and he tried down, but they were there as well. They pushed closer, caging him in, until he felt like it was inevitable that both he and his vessel would be ripped apart by the continuous spray of bullets. He found it hard to think that he would die to the bars of his cage.

As the planes came close enough that he could hear the explosion of the gunpowder in the barrels, he heard the zoom of another vessel overhead. He looked, but saw nothing, and then presumed that it was just another Nightmare. Then it passed again, but this time it came with a stream of bullets of its own. Jacob winced, thinking the cage had just been given a lid, but he heard the sound of an explosion outside, and opened his eyes in time to see one of the Brigade's aircraft hurtling downwards in a stream of smoke and flames.

The remaining Nightmares broke apart, turning to their attacker, which Jacob noted with a hint of pride, and then a lot of worry, had the number fourteen on its tail. Whistler turned sharply and came around, head on, blasting his guns, until a second Nightmare tumbled from the sky. He might not have been trigger-happy, but when he fired, he hit his target. He faced them like they were not flying arsenals, but nothing more than bad dreams.

Jacob tried to gain ground as he saw the other two vessels locking onto Whistler's plane from below and behind, but he feared he would not get there in time, or that his gunfire would miss the mark. Then the radio crackled, and he heard the clipped voice of Rommond, and the cackle of Armax, until he saw his comrades, human and maran, zooming by, blasting the nearest attacker apart, and tearing a hole in the wing of the remaining fighter.

"Phew!" Jacob cried, saluting the airborne cavalry.

But he spoke too soon. The smoke cleared a little, and the last of the fighter planes, engulfed in flames, came towards them. They broke apart again, but the fighter picked the closest target and turned his fireball towards it with the determination of the vengeful dead.

Chapter Nineteen

A LONG WAY DOWN

They watched in horror as the left wing of Markus' plane broke apart. They heard his voice for a moment, a stutter of panic, silenced by static. The nose of the biplane dipped suddenly, and the vehicle plunged towards the ground.

"My son!" Trokus screamed.

"Eject!" Rommond cried over the radio.

"I can't!" Markus exclaimed. They heard him frantically bashing buttons. They could hear his breath, his panic, his terror. Every sound was magnified through the lens of fear.

In that split second of a moment, when the teen's brief life must have been flashing swiftly before his eyes, Jacob could see the two potential outcomes: the one where Markus could not get out in time, and died; and the one where he managed to eject, but broke his back in the process, and spent the rest of his life paralysed, cared for by his loving mother and father, whose bodies were intact, but whose hearts were broken.

The plane hurtled past Jacob's position, and as it fell, he could see Markus inside the bubble of glass, his hands pressed against the pane, pushing and shoving, trying to get it open. It was a harrowing sight, just as the sounds were distressing. It was easier to know that someone was dying elsewhere than to watch and hear them falling towards their doom.

"Markus!" Trokus roared. In the anguish of that shout, Jacob could hear the love the Regime commander had for his son, and the loss it would mean. Though Jacob had heard the sounds of Markus careening towards death, he heard in Trokus that a part of him was falling too.

There was a moment when there was no sound, which was very noticeable after all the shouts and pants and thumps of before. Then they heard the radio crackle on, and the voice was muted, but it was unmistakable.

"Goodbye, dad," Markus said, faint and afraid. "Tell mom I love her. T-tell Jaycie I'll miss her."

Maybe Trokus said something in response, but they did not hear it. Maybe he roared again, or cried, or thumped the dashboard, or pleaded with gods, or prayed to devils.

"There's nothing we can do," Rommond said coolly. It was a rehearsed line, the kind a general was trained to give. And for Rommond, it was a tired line, one he had given too many times before. "We have to stick to the mission." Another line from the book. *The greater good.* None of it mattered to those suffering what was to them the greatest evil.

Jacob shook his head. He had no words to give. The little gesture he gave was its own kind of prayer, its own kind of eulogy. It said all it needed to. Markus was just sixteen. *Hell, still a boy*, Jacob thought. *Barely older than Whistler.* The loss was greater for the young. But war had no sympathy for them. Death did not discriminate. It sought them all.

Then something caught his eye, and he watched in shock and awe as another plane began to dive. He thought it was another hit, another crumbling frame, but as he looked down he saw that the plane was intact. He could not see the pilot inside, but he could see the numbers painted on the tail fin. Fourteen.

No, Jacob thought. *What are you doing?* He hoped the number was not an omen, that the tail fin would not become a gravestone. *Here lies Whistler. Only fourteen years old.*

"Where's he going?" Armax asked.

"Stick to the plan," Rommond urged them. "We all die if that bomb goes off."

Jacob shook his head again, hoping it was not another eulogy. He kept his eyes level, watching the path through the clouds ahead. His heart thumped, and his mind nagged at him. He felt he had a promise to keep.

He could no longer avert his eyes. He glanced down, struggling with his belt to get a better view. Much of his sight was blocked by his own vessel, but he saw Whistler diving straight down towards the spiralling descent of Markus' plane.

What is *he doing?* Jacob wondered. It did not look like a rescue mission. It looked like suicide. Whistler's plane dived so fast that it was quickly out of view, but it resurfaced soon after, below the falling, burning wreck. It then became clear what he was trying to do: he was trying to catch him as he fell.

Hell, Jacob thought. He dived straight down, hoping he would make it in time, and hoping he would not just add to the mess. It was one man down, but now it might be three. If people kept trying to save them, there would be no one left to stop the Worldwaker. He was thankful then that Rommond's grim determination was as strong as ever.

Jacob's plane hurtled down, faster than he expected, and yet not fast enough to avoid seeing Whistler try to pass beneath Markus and slow his descent. The boy struggled with the catch. The other plane fell too quickly, and the smoke obscured his vision.

At last Jacob came beneath both of the other planes, but he knew it was impossible to slow or save Markus from there. With just one wing, the youth's plane spun madly as it fell. They needed it to fall straight, or glide, or do anything a little bit more predictable if they had any hope of saving him.

"We need to break the other wing," Jacob said, well aware that the boy's father was also listening, and also praying. "We need to stop it spinning."

"It's too risky," Rommond replied. "You're trying to catch a fireball and hoping you won't get burnt. Get back up here. It's over."

Trokus must have realised it too. He had overseen many test flights, and many failures. Aircraft of this kind were still very new to the world of Altadas, and pioneers risked their lives at every turn. Whistler and Jacob were not pioneers, but were risking their lives all the same.

"No!" Whistler said. "We have to try!"

He fired at Markus' spinning craft, destroying the second wing, and stabilising its descent. The smoke still obscured their view, but they could see Markus unconscious inside, drooping in his seat.

That's going to make this harder, Jacob thought.

The smuggler dived further, matching the speed of Markus' vessel, coming beneath the body, and pushing the reinforced wings of his own craft against the wheels of the other. The sound of screeching blasted his eardrums, and his plane rocked violently as he tried to stop the steep descent. For a moment it seemed like it was working, and Jacob was able to pull up a little, enough to wonder what in God's name he would need to do next.

Keep it steady, he urged himself. *You can do this, Jacob*. He had never lied so convincingly to himself before.

Then gravity intervened, and the wheels of Markus' monoplane skidded off the wings, and the vessel plummeted like a bullet. Whistler turned sharply and tried one last-ditch effort to save Markus, but he could not get there in time. The other vessel made its final fall, exploding as it hit the earth.

Jacob sighed and shook his head. It was almost worse to nearly make it, and have victory snatched away at the last moment. The fates were cruel. He could almost hear their laughter from the clouds.

There was a moment where Whistler circled the crash site, clearly not knowing what to do. When Jacob pulled up to rejoin the others, Whistler followed.

"I tried," the boy sobbed.

"You did good, kid," Jacob said.

"But I didn't save him."

"We can't save them all," Rommond replied. Jacob thought it likely the general had spoken that into a mirror many times before.

Trokus was silent. Maybe he was thankful that they had tried, but he could not be thankful that they had failed. He would find it difficult to explain the loss to his wife, and to explain to his daughter why she no longer had a big brother. Jacob thought it was probably easier not to explain, to just not go back at all.

"I know this is a great loss," Rommond said, "but think of the rest of your family, Commander. The mission is bigger than all of us. The bomb is bigger than all of us."

There was no time to grieve, for up ahead, as if summoned by the general's words, they saw the large frame of the Dreamdevil, and beneath its belly, attached with bolts and wires, the bulbous hulk of the Worldwaker.

Chapter Twenty

THE IRON RALLY

Brooklyn and Alex hiked the hill overlooking Dunedale, and were amazed at the sight. The many tightly-packed old buildings were draped with humongous banners and flags, many with the emblem of the Regime, and many more with the icon of the Iron Emperor. There were statues of him everywhere, finely carved from iron, unlike the crude representations in the Dune Burrows, and they towered over everyone present, reminding them of who their ruler was, and what they sought in Altadas.

A giant platform extended over the crowd, bobbing up and down as a mix of downward-facing propellers and upwards-pulling dirigibles kept it just above the tallest person's reach. Just above. Close enough to almost touch, but far enough to never achieve.

The crowd was huge, filling every square inch of the many winding streets, and every doorway, and every window, and every balcony. It seemed that the entire city's inhabitants were out there, and maybe those of other cities too. It was a dangerous thing *not* to be out there, for it suggested that they had something to hide.

There was tension among the people, and the chatter was low. Even from their height, Brooklyn and Alex could tell that the people spoke only of the Iron Emperor. *Will he show? What will he say?*

Brooklyn had different questions in mind: *Should we be here? Is it safe?*

The wait was agonising, fuelled by the common cloud of apprehension that hung above the city mob. They came not with pitchforks, but with salutes. They did not come to bash and burn, but to cheer and caw. It was a riot of enthusiasm, and yet the longer it took for the inciter to arrive, the more it seemed like it might be a riot of a different kind. He was their drug as much as their drug-pusher. To them, he was Hope, and the giver of Hope.

A step. A general came out. Then another. The crowd grew silent. Even the wind seemed to stop to listen. A stream of high-ranking soldiers came out one-by-one, as orderly as their uniforms, and Brooklyn could not help but think that Rommond would have approved. Yet this was not just a display of order; it was a display of might and power.

Then *he* entered. The Iron Emperor.

Brooklyn could almost hear the catching of breaths. Several people fainted in the crowd, and were left to lay where they dropped. Those who might have caught them were enraptured by the sight of their leader, so rarely seen by them, and so often dreamed of. Yet if this was a dream, it was one they did not want to wake from.

He was tall and of average build, with black hair combed neatly to the side. He was not as attractive as the statues made out, but he exuded charisma in a difficult to describe way. His very stance and posture had presence, as if he was more than just a man, more than just a maran. He wore a black trench coat over a black uniform, and the black was like the perfect pitch of the starry night. He wore the universe as a garment, and it fit him well, and not even the breeze seemed to dare move it.

His cleanly-shaven face was like granite, like a statue of its own. He stood silent and still, and basked in the moment, and made the people bask in it too. If he breathed, no one heard the breath. If he blinked, no one saw his eyes shut. He watched them, and though he looked at none of them, he saw them all. His eyes were like galaxies, and everyone could get lost in them. How many stars flickered there, no one knew, but every time he glanced upon someone, a new star ignited, a new star was caught in the gravity of his stare.

The soldiers on stage with him stood far behind. None dared defy his height. From the perfect angle, which was the angle aimed at all, they looked minuscule compared to him. Yet though they were dwarfed by him, their very presence on the same stage as him elevated them, like mere men become gods, transfigured by the greatest god of all.

His shadow was immense, covering many at the front of the crowd. Though they stood in his darkness, they felt like they stood in his light.

He stirred but an inch, and the audience gasped. The performance was about to begin, and the people who had paid with their self-sufficiency and self-thinking pulled their eyelids open wide so that they could assimilate it all. They looked on as one, and felt as one, and waited as one. He raised the index finger of his right hand, and all eyes followed.

"We," he said, his voice thick and deep, sonorous and soothing, "the greatest people of all nations, of all worlds, of all peoples, and all powers, came here to this nation, to this world, to these people, and these powers, and like we have always done, we came and conquered."

The audience cheered, until he silenced them with his hand.

"Though the great stand before you, the great times are still ahead. Altadas has awoken. Our people have awoken. No longer will we be the victims of illness. We will conquer it. No longer will we be the victims of death. We will conquer that too."

Another round of cheers from the harmonious choir, as perfectly in time when they stopped at his bidding as they did at their starting.

"I know your sorrow. I know your struggle. I feel it. I feel it for you. All that I do, I do for you. All that I am, I am for you. I take upon this burden of leadership, that I might lead us on to victory, victory against all odds, against all that assail us. It is a mighty burden, held only by the mighty, and yet I do not baulk at the task. I hold it willingly."

They applauded his great self-sacrifice.

"So too must you become willing participants in this greater struggle, and though you cannot support what only the mighty can hold, you can support the mighty. You can hold up the mighty in your eyes, and in your minds, and in your hearts."

They held him up, and it was no burden to them.

"Our fight goes beyond mere man and woman. Our fight goes beyond mere mortal. We fight so that there may be no more fighting. We battle so that there may be no more war. It is a fight that brought us through many worlds, and may bring us to many more, for there is nothing, no barrier, no wall, that will stand in our way. We do this not just for ourselves, but for all peoples, for it is only when the natural order of things is restored, when we once again have our rightful place in the hierarchy of all things, that everyone will have peace. For, my people, my comrades, the universe has the same sickness our people do, and we must not just find the cure for ourselves, but *be* the cure for everyone else."

They sought earnestly to find and be the cure.

"You must obey," he told them, and his eyes fixed on them seemingly one by one, like a spotlight. "You must submit. You must follow. It is a necessary thing. It is an overwhelming thing. For, to restore the natural order of things above, we must restore it here below. The leaders will lead, and the followers will follow. Then there is no chaos, and when there is no chaos, there is no room for illness to breed. For, you see, disobedience is an illness of the mind. Disloyalty is an illness of the heart. Defiance is an illness of the soul."

They reflected on their ailments, and sought to rid themselves of them.

"Look about you," he told them, and for the first time since he stepped on stage, they took their eyes off him. "Look at our numbers. Look at the pageantry. Look at the landships lined up. Look at this mere example of our might and our majesty."

As he spoke, Brooklyn spotted several aeroplanes in the sky, speeding swiftly towards the city. Even at this vantage point, he could tell they were his designs. He could feel the stirring of the machine spirits. He could almost feel Rommond up there too.

"Even now, look above you," the Iron Emperor commanded, "and you will see our latest arsenal." His voice boomed over the microphone, a weapon of its own. "We conquered land and water before, and now we have conquered the skies."

The cheers were ear-rending, and they were uniform. Not the maddened frenzy of a worked-up crowd, but the zealous cries of followers, all speaking with one voice, chanting the same slogan, the same words, carefully selected by the Iron Emperor himself.

Conquer, they cried. *Cure*, they hollered.

He thumped his chest and raised his fist, and without any order, or any direction, the entire crowd gave the Regime salute. He did it again, more forcefully, and they repeated the gesture with more enthusiasm. Again he drove his fist into the sky, with anger and passion, and they became angry and passionate in their salutes.

He was not a puppet-master, pulling the strings of the unwilling. They made the strings themselves, and gave them to him. They gave them to him for safe-keeping. They trusted him with their lives, with their thoughts, with everything. They would live through him, and only him, and so get to experience a sliver of his godliness, which they could only ever aspire to reaching out to. He was more than them, more than all of them, and they had to give up their identity and individuality to become a part of him. He was the greater good. Nothing else mattered, and when they looked upon him, and baulked beneath his mighty shadow, they did not want anything else.

The Iron Emperor left the stage, and the army cleared the crowd, making way for a modified black warwagon with an open roof. The great leader with no name sat inside it, waving to the cheering crowd. It drove on through the streets, and people followed, and musicians played, and dancers danced, and soldiers marched. The parade proceeded down the street, and though at a glance it seemed like everyone there was full of elation, to Brooklyn it almost looked like it was staged. The music dropped just in time for a wild applause. The cart halted just where a child was ready to give her leader a white flower. Everything went like clockwork. What the Iron Emperor willed, happened.

The warwagon passed them by, and for the briefest of moments, Brooklyn thought that the Iron Emperor looked up at him. He felt a sudden panic, as if all his fears had been laid bare. Every barrier he erected was broken in that short glance, every supporting cliff ripped away from his straining fingers. He was naked, and he was falling, and there was nowhere to hide, and no one to catch him.

"Are you okay?" Alex asked. "You look a little … pale."

Brooklyn regained his senses, but he still felt as

though he was being watched.

"I think it's time to go," he said.

"Right you are!"

"And I think this last part of my journey, I must make alone."

"Are you sure? Do you know the w-w-way?"

"Too well," Brooklyn said, holding up his metal hand. "It is not far from here where I was made."

Chapter Twenty-one

THE WINGWALKERS

As the Regime and Resistance planes approached the Dreamdevil, it became clear that there would be another problem. On the giant wings of the aeroplane, men and women walked to and fro, as if they were unaware that they were thousands of feet up in the air. More of them clambered out of a hatch on top of the plane, racing up a small ladder placed precariously at the front of the wings. They all had backpacks on, but they did not contain parachutes. They contained wings.

"Hell," Jacob said. "And I thought flying *inside* this thing was bad enough."

One of the wingwalkers pulled down sharply on the strings attached to his backpack, and the wooden wings unfurled. They opened out like one of the fans used by the royalty of old, thin wooden slats held together with paper. The wings did not look any more durable.

It seemed as though the aerial daredevils were preparing to leap off, but Rommond pushed open the glass canopy of his plane, stood up, and pointed his pistol at one of the wingwalkers. He fired, and the man stumbled backwards off the wing, plummeting

133

to the ground.

Rommond ducked back inside to stabilise his aircraft, pulling the canopy door shut. As he did so, Armax opened fire on the wingwalkers on the other wing, using the monoplane's built-in machine guns. The bullets struck several wingwalkers, but they also struck the wing and hull of the plane itself.

"For God's sake, don't shoot!" Rommond cried. "The last thing we need right now is a spray of bullets flying towards that bomb."

"But you just—"

"I know what I did, and I know what I'm doing," Rommond barked. "If you can fire a perfect shot with a pistol, then fire away. Otherwise, keep your gun muzzled, and your mouth too."

The moment came, and the first of the wingwalkers leapt off. Some dove, opening their wings as they fell, while others let the wind catch their already unfurled feathers, drifting and floating with the aerial tide.

"Here they come," Jacob said.

One of the wingwalkers raced towards him, but he turned sharply to get out of the way. He could see others heading for the other planes, but his mirror showed that his own attacker was also turning to catch him.

Jacob veered right, then left, but the wingwalker was more agile than his aircraft, following it with ease. While he turned sharply, his assailant turned agilely, and it was clear from the controlled folding and unfurling of the wooden feathers that the Armageddon Brigade had tested them thoroughly.

The wingwalker closed on him, so much so that

he could see the man's grin in the mirror. Then he heard the cheer of Armax on the radio, and saw his comrade fly his plane straight into the wingwalker, crushing it like a fly against a windscreen.

"Too easy!" Armax boasted. "You should've made windshield wipers on these!"

As Jacob dove, he saw another wingwalker diving towards Whistler's plane, but the boy performed a swift barrel roll to avoid it, and it flew onwards to seek out an easier target. Then another came, this time from the side, but Whistler performed another roll, striking the aerial acrobat with the wing of his plane. The man fell, dazed, and his feathers fluttered and broke apart in his descent. Yet Whistler had little time to celebrate, for another wingwalker managed to land upon the edge of his wing. He tumbled again, but the wingwalker held on, and the boy was getting dizzy.

"Hold on, kid," Jacob said over the radio as he flew down to slightly above the same height. He could see Whistler looking back at him, and looking anxiously at the wingwalker clambering up the wing. He turned sharply on his side, sending the attacker sliding down, but he never tumbled off, always seizing the edge just in time. Yet this constant throwing helped bide the boy some time as Jacob's aeroplane approached.

"He won't fall off," Whistler said.

"I'll need you to keep it steady," Jacob replied.

"I'm trying to shake him!"

"Don't."

Whistler must have had a lot of trust in Jacob, because he immediately steadied his aircraft, giving the wingwalker a level footing towards the cockpit. The man closed up his wings and ran, but even as he neared the glass canopy, Jacob's plane flew in, and the wing narrowly passed over the airfoil of Whistler's vessel, knocking the wingwalker off. They watched as he tried to open his feathers in the drop, but plummeted instead.

Armax loved the chase, and loved this one more than the last, because he got to see the terror in the enemy's face as he dived right into them. He used the radio as his own personal kill list, applauding his every victory, and cheering those of companions.

Then one of the wingwalkers landed on Armax's plane, but before the attacker could do anything, the pilot opened the canopy and grabbed the wingwalker by the leg, knocking him from his feet. With one hand still firmly on the controls, he pulled the man closer and wrapped his arm around his neck. It was difficult to kick and fight, and Armax had a powerful grip. He squeezed until the man fell unconscious, then tore the backpack from him, before letting him tumble off the edge.

"This'll come in handy," he said, closing the canopy.

Great, Jacob thought. *Why didn't Brooklyn have designs for these too?* Yet he did not quite think he had the guts to learn how to fly with his own wings. He knew he was much more of an expert at falling.

Even as it looked like the battle against the wing-walkers was succeeding, another set climbed out of the Dreamdevil, and these wore larger backpacks, and seemed to wear armour as well as wings.

"Looks like we have some heavies," Armax said with glee.

The wingwalkers dove, but they did not spread out. They travelled together, forming a ring as they went, and aimed straight for Rommond's monoplane, like a bullet from his own gun. He dodged and dove, but he could not avoid them all, nor could he perform Whistler's tricks, for fear that striking the heavy suits of his assailants might damage his own wings.

"I can't lose them," the general said.

"Now can we shoot?" Armax asked.

"No," Rommond replied, a little more resigned than usual. The heavies landed, attaching ropes and wires. "Stay on target. Find a way onboard."

Jacob pushed on, but even as he did, he saw the new wingwalkers taking out what looked like small bombs from their backpacks. Rommond opened the canopy and fired at two of the wingwalkers, but the glass bubble acted as a shield for those behind. No amount of trick shots were going to work. Nothing would bounce off the clouds.

The bombs were set in place, and the wingwalkers dived off. They did not seek out new targets, as most of the other planes were now out of reach. Yet, soon after they pulled their parachutes, Armax came by at great speed, slicing through the parachute wires with the wings of his plane. The wingwalkers fell, but their fall came too late.

Rommond opened the canopy again and tried to dislodge one of the bombs with his hand, ever mindful that at any moment it could rip off his entire arm. He managed to loosen one, which then slipped away as he shook the plane, igniting in the empty air. But there were many of them, and some were stuck on tight. He could hear them ticking away.

He closed the canopy, like the lid of a coffin. "Stay on target," he repeated with a stifled sigh. Everyone stayed on target, but all eyes were on his plane.

The explosions were blinding. In the flash of fire and light, there were many metal and wooden splinters. As it subsided, Jacob watched in horror as the wingless husk of Rommond's plane plummeted down, still burning, like a comet, to the ground.

Chapter Twenty-two

HELD

The Hold was a prison network of five separate buildings, stretched across the desert of Altadas like a giant hand. Prisoners were kept in different parts depending on how valuable they were, and moved around periodically to prevent breakout or capture by the enemy. Rescuing Mudro from the Hold was one thing—they had to find out which part he was in first.

"It's doubtful they brought him to the Thumb," Taberah said. By the time she returned with Gouet, Tardo was ready to broadcast. "We raided that before to free Brogan and Jacob. It's the closest to Resistance territory, so it's an easy target."

"Well, that still leaves four options," Leadman replied.

"That's where this guy comes in." Taberah held a gun to the head of one of the communications agents kept alive at Commspire Oasis.

"We're good to go," Tardo said, hovering a finger over the broadcast button.

"Stick to the script," Taberah warned the agent.

The radio croaked on.

"Oasis h-here," the agent stammered.

"Command receiving."

The agent's nervousness was palpable, and—worse—audible. "We, eh … intercepted a … a call."

Taberah nodded at Tardo and ran her finger swiftly across her throat. He muted the microphone.

"Keep it natural," Taberah urged the agent, lowering her gun a little. "Pretend."

"Come in, Oasis," the radio crackled.

"Sorry about that," the agent continued. The hesitation was still there, but he covered it better. "Bit of a sandstorm here. Lots of interference. We intercepted a communication from the Resistance. Turns out they're trying to free the Magus."

"Copy that. Have you got details?"

"Nothing concrete, but it seems like they're bringing an army. You better move him to a more secure location."

"He's already in the Little Finger."

Taberah scribbled a note for the agent and pointed to it.

"It's likely they have some intel that he's there. We need to move him quick."

"Copy that. We'll wheel him out."

The conversation ended, and Tardo gave a nod and a hearty smile. He was real Resistance material now.

"You did good," Taberah told the agent. "And I'm feeling generous. When we have our man, you can walk free."

The agent breathed again.

"Getting soft?" Leadman said, before unloading a bullet in the agent's head.

Taberah glared at him. "Just saving my bullets for the real battle."

The real battle came swiftly enough. Now that they knew Mudro had been kept in the Little Finger, they raced along the dirt tracks to intercept the transport leaving that location. They had to be quick or Mudro would be moved off the main road and down one of the paths to the Index, Middle, or Ring. At that stage, they would have lost their opportunity.

They parked out of sight at the top of a dune overlooking the road, and waited. In time, Leadman's spyglass showed a warwagon, accompanied by two Moving Castles, coming down the road.

"It's time," he said.

The vehicles neared, and the Resistance forces began their assault. The Silver Ghost charged forward, and the bulldozer landship opened fire. One of the Moving Castles collapsed in flames, while the Silver Ghost drove straight into the other, knocking it to the ground and scattering the gunners from the crenellations.

As Taberah and Gouet opened fire from the windows of the Silver Ghost, changing position to get a better shot, Leadman's landship drove straight into the fleeing warwagon, knocking it to its side, before blasting a hole in the bottom.

Guards fled, but did not flee faster than bullets. Then out of the haze of dust and rubble stepped Doctor Mudro, dusting off his cobalt waistcoat.

"Finally," he said. "I was beginning to wish I'd studied escapology."

"You should have studied it anyway while you were behind bars," Gouet said, stepping out of the Silver Ghost with Taberah.

"Gouet!" Mudro exclaimed. "I thought you were dead."

"Sure, I'm close enough, amn't I? Got both feet in the grave at this stage."

"In this war," Mudro said, with a wave of his hand, "don't we all?" He paused. "Now, before we continue … neither of you would happen to have a pipe and some leaf? The guards disposed of mine."

Gouet gave a cackle, and looked at Taberah. "I told you he'd be desperate for a puff." He took a little box out of his robes and handed it to Mudro.

"Much obliged, good sir," the doctor said, taking the pipe out of the box and quickly stuffing it. "Hmm, a light?"

Gouet scoffed. "Come now, you're not that weakened by the air of this world."

Mudro sighed. He held his right hand over the open end of the pipe, whispered something while it was still in his mouth, and clicked his fingers over the weed. It did not sound like a normal click. They heard it with something other than their ears.

A sizzle of smoke rose like a pillar from the pipe.

"Or maybe you are," Gouet said. "You used to be good with fire."

"You used to be good with water," Mudro replied. "Where's the rain?"

Gouet waved his hand dismissively at the doctor, and grumbled as he headed back to the Silver Ghost.

"Good to see you repairing that friendship,"

Taberah said.

"Some things aren't so easily forgotten."

"What about the Memory Magus?"

"Ha! It's easy to forget the old world when you bring in the new. Or, as Gouet might say, it's easy to forget, full stop. Now, before I do, where's Haladon? I presume you mean to get us all together?"

"He's dead," Taberah said. "The Regime found him. We lost a huge supply of amulets."

"And a life," Mudro pointed out.

"We lose those all the time."

"If there's only two of us left, that doesn't bode well for the amulet business. You know I've never been much good with them. And Gouet's not exactly going to be in business much longer himself. What then?"

Taberah shrugged. "We better hope more of your kind are exiled here."

"Seems like it's been a while since we heard of a new landing."

"Some say the Regime released creatures into the water to stop the ships from reaching the shore."

"Some say a lot of things. Is it true?"

"It doesn't matter," Taberah said. "We're ending this once and for all now. No more blocking the birth channels. It's time we reclaim that territory."

"With Gouet here, I had a feeling you were going to say that."

"A premonition?"

"More like a memory, repeating itself."

"It won't be like last time."

"Yes, because there are less of us now."

"I mean, we'll find them."

"And if we do?"

"We fight them."

"If we were back in Iraldas, I would be up for anything," Mudro said, waving his hand towards the west, as if that land was just out of view, "but here, the rules are different. Magic doesn't work the same here. The more stark the machinery, the more subtle the magic." He paused for a moment. "Speaking of which … have you got my gear?"

"It's in the Ghostch—the Silver Ghost."

The smoke from Mudro's pipe lingered a little longer than usual. "I guess it's the Ghostchaser again."

"But we're not chasing ghosts this time."

"Aren't we?"

She looked at him, and he looked right through her.

"Who's your guide?" he asked.

She did not hold his gaze. "I don't know what you mean."

"You didn't just stumble upon the location of the Birth-masters. We gave up that search a long time ago. What changed?"

"The war changed."

"The war is always changing. Something changed with you."

"I realised where my battle lies."

"You didn't realise that on your own," he pointed out. "Who's your guide?"

"Don't tell him," Elizah said, just to her. "He'll think you're crazy."

"It's just a hunch," Taberah said at last.

"Well, I have a hunch that it's something more."

"You're wrong, Mudro."

Mudro raised an eyebrow. "I hope I am, Taberah. I hope I am."

Chapter Twenty-three

BOARDING THE BOMB

Jacob flew his plane over the Dreamdevil, struggling to get a good view of where he could possibly land when he eventually leapt out. The idea sounded more insane now than it had before—and it was madness then. Rommond seemed so confident about it, but he was gone now, and the confidence of all went with him. Yet the mission lived on, and the general's passing might not have been in vain if the survivors found a way to succeed, to make survivors out of everyone else.

"I can't get a clear view," Jacob spoke into the radio. "I can see up and to the sides, but not down." People used to say *when up at great heights, never look down*. Maybe there was a good reason for that design.

"Try this," Whistler replied, and Jacob saw the boy's plane fly over him—upside down. He looked up, and clearly saw Whistler's smiling face and waving hand. He waved back, but doubted he would be smiling if he could dare find the courage for such a move. Yet he had to find it somewhere. *Hopefully not the afterlife.*

He flew on, and turned around for another pass, this time a little higher than before. He felt he needed the extra height, in case he accidentally drooped down when the world was spinning. He took a deep breath, and let it out swiftly with a sigh.

"Here goes then," he said to himself, before turning the steering stick sharply to the right. The plane turned, and kept turning, but then it seemed like the world turned instead, and he saw the land tumbling away, as if it was falling into the sky. He felt a sudden nausea, and his head hurt, and his eyes blurred a little as they tried to adjust to a scene that did not make any sense.

He felt the tug of gravity, pulling him towards the new sand-covered sky. His seat belt dug into his abdomen, and the straps around his shoulders clung to him tightly like a frightful friend. The glass of the canopy was so clear, and offered such a great peripheral view, that it almost felt like there was nothing there at all.

He passed over the Dreamdevil, slowing the engine, hoping to get as best a view as he could. He saw the giant wingspan, the smoke stack, the tail fin, the ropes that held things together, and all the polished curves, which would not hold a footfall.

He flinched as another plane passed between him and the Dreamdevil, upright, and yet looking like it was upside down. He could see Armax inside, strapping his wingwalker backpack on, and Jacob could not help but wish that he had one of his own.

He turned his plane upright, taking one final look at his target. The best place to land seemed like the wings themselves, where the wingwalkers had previously perched, making it look like solid ground.

But it was one thing to leap *from* the wings compared to leaping *to* them.

He reached towards the backpack at his feet. It had a parachute inside, and two grappling guns attached to the outside. *Everything you need to commit suicide*, Jacob thought. He had to remind himself of the bomb, and Rommond's last words, to find the courage deep inside himself. He never really found it, but he found purpose. He had a mission. He had to see it through.

He passed around again, and pushed open the canopy. The wind was fierce now. It grabbed his hair and pulled at his goggles. The sound of it clattered off his ears, until he could barely hear himself think.

He checked his equipment, especially his backpack, hoping the parachute was in working order. There was no way to test it. *Hell*, he thought, *no one wants to test if it works*. If it failed, it was already too late.

He unbuckled his seat belt. Now that it came to it, his heart banged a vicious beat, as if it had to live out all its last moments right then and there, and could not beat fast enough to live them all. He gripped the side of the cockpit, and felt the shudder in his hand. With his other hand, he tried to keep his plane steady as he stood up, but it rocked in sympathy with him.

He was a decent shot, but he never fired himself at a target—and *decent* did not seem quite good enough. Yet the moment of his calculations was approaching, and he knew that the Dreamdevil would pass beneath him any second now. If he missed his opportunity, it would only get harder to conquer his fleeting nerves.

Jacob leapt, and had to fight against the impulse

to close his eyes. The wind stole his breath, and while the ground was still very far away, it threatened to steal his life. He saw his plane veering away of its own accord, and dipping, and then diving. There was only one way for it to go without a pilot, and that was down. He just hoped he would not follow suit.

He saw someone else leaping, but in the flurry of the fall he could not see who it was. They struck the edge, and slipped, and cascaded off like rain. Their scream was not familiar, so he presumed it was one of Trokus' men. His voice followed his body to the depths below. If he pulled his parachute, Jacob could not tell, for he had his own fall to worry about, and had to fight the urge to pull the strings of his own.

It all passed in a moment, and suddenly the stark yellow wing was beneath him, and he grunted as he struck the metal. Then it seemed that his landing pad was moving away from him, and he felt himself sliding across the wing. He reached out with sweaty palms, and kicked his leather boots against the hull, but he only added extra noises to his slide.

He slipped off the edge of the wing, but reached for his back and fired one of the grappling hooks ahead. It must have been a lucky shot—or a desperate one—because it wrapped around one of the metal poles attaching the upper wings to the lower ones. He swung for a moment left and right, until gravity tugged him towards the hull. He clung with all his might, well aware that his strength would fade over time, and that the sweat on his hands would build, and that he had no idea how he would get from that precarious position to the safety of inside.

* * *

Armax threw open the canopy of his craft and leapt out without looking. He immediately opened the wings on his backpack, and the wind caught him and tugged him upwards.

"Whoa!" he cried, trying to steady himself. The wind robbed the word on its way from his mouth to his ears, and its thieving fingers tried to take him too.

He drifted down before he realised there were handles made into some of the wooden feathers, catering for different arm lengths, allowing him to grab hold and make the wings an extension of him. He used these to turn, gliding more effortlessly, then flapped his arms to help him gain height. It was remarkably easier than he expected it to be, an intuitive system, though from the vantage point of others, he looked like a rather clumsy bird.

He made for the giant wings of the Dreamdevil, and tried to pull his own wings closed as his feet skirted the surface, but he found this a lot more difficult, for he had to fight against the brawn of the breeze, which tugged him off the edge. He dropped a little, and felt the hot steam of the smoke shaft as the biplane passed beneath him, and the steam pushed him up again, and pulled him back towards the rear of the aircraft. The Dreamdevil moved so quickly that the tail fin swiftly came towards him, like the fin of the shark-emblazoned bomb, and struck his left leg, breaking the bone and sending him spinning away.

* * *

Jacob struggled to hold on to the hull of the aeroplane, the wind lashing him, the breeze bashing him. The aerodynamic curves of the vessel made it difficult to get a firm grip anywhere—and easy to slip off. Though his boots had grips, there was nothing to grip too, so he was forced to haul his entire weight with his hands.

For a moment he thought he might be able to reach back to grab the other grappling gun, but that meant letting go with one hand. It was not just fear that stopped him. He knew he could not hold his weight with a single, slippery grip.

He saw Armax flying around the Dreamdevil, struggling to land, and what envy he had of his companion's wings quickly faded when he saw him sucked away by the cyclone of steam.

Nissi jumped down, making a roll as she struck the wing, before firing her grappling hook and leaping off the edge, swinging down onto the hull. Everything appeared so effortless that it seemed like she might single-handedly hijack the Dreamdevil and disarm the Worldwaker.

She was so focused on the mission—without doubt one of Rommond's own—that she paid no heed to Jacob's struggle on the other side, but leapt and jumped and danced her way across the vessel until she arrived near the main doorway inside. She fired another grappling hook to a beam jutting out above the door, and tied the other end to her belt. Then she pulled the door open, dangled in front of it, and cast a smoke cylinder inside, before throwing herself in after.

At that moment, Trokus' plane pulled as close to the Dreamdevil as possible, and the commander handed over the steering to the gunner, who had so much experience flying that he could keep the wings almost perfectly level, steady enough for Trokus to walk across like a ramp to the door. He jumped the final gap, and almost missed his mark. Nissi pulled his dangling legs into the haze.

Jacob clambered up the rope, wrapping it around his arm as he went, and pushing his feet against the oily hull to give him some extra support. As he got closer to the grappling hook, he could see its clutch around the pole was precarious. The more he pulled on it, the more its metal fingers opened.

Hang in there, he urged, as much an injunction for himself as that weakening iron grip.

He reached the top, just as it looked like the hook was about to give way, and threw his arms around the metal pole. He paused there for a moment, catching his breath, though the wind made it difficult to catch.

When he calmed himself just a little, for there were many more reasons to not be calm, he reached out for the next support pole, and found it several feet outside his grasp. He could not hold onto one and grab the other. He had to let go first.

He waited for the plane to steady just a little, then raced towards the pole ahead, hugging it like he hugged the last. He repeated this several more times, until he neared the front of the lower wings, and the ladder that led up to the top, where there was a hatch leading into the cockpit. He could have made his way around to the back, where Nissi and Trokus had entered, but that was a longer journey, and he would need the second grappling gun for that. He had not enjoyed the use of the first. He thought small steps suited him better this far up. It was better than giant leaps.

He climbed up the ladder, and felt it rock beneath his weight. He wished it was anchored better, but the wind made the most stable structures shudder. He reached the top, and grabbed hold of the handle on the hatch. He tugged, but it would not budge. His plan did not seem so good any more. He clung to the handle now for support, kneeling on the roof of the Dreamdevil, feeling as helpless as ever. He felt like he might have to wait there until Nissi and Trokus cleared out the plane, and broke into the cockpit—if they even made it that far.

Suddenly the hatch door opened and pushed forward, and the force of the push sent Jacob flying. He tumbled down onto the windscreen, and flayed madly to get a grip. He glanced behind him and saw the spinning propeller slicing through the air. The nose sloped down into this rotating death trap, and Jacob would have already been sliding were it not for the momentum of the craft keeping him pinned to the window. If it slowed even a little, momentum might lose its brief war with gravity and let him slip down to his doom. He hugged the glass and closed his eyes, trying not to think about it, yet thinking of nothing else. When he dared to open them again, he saw the pilots inside the Dreamdevil staring at him, and was shocked to see that Cala was in there too.

Chapter Twenty-four

LANDLOCKED

"Thanks for your help," Taberah said.

"Dumping me so soon?" Leadman asked. "Now I know how Jacob feels."

She struggled to hide her irritation. "You might have seen a lot of war, but you won't have seen anything like what we'll be facing. Landships won't be any use. Soldiers won't be either. That's why I need the Magi."

"And I was looking forward to killing some Birth-masters," Leadman said, feigning disappointment.

"Maybe look forward to leading the victors instead."

He smiled broadly, which, with his great jaw, was very broad indeed. "So Rommond told you, eh? Well, I suppose it's best that more people know. Just in case, you know, the old Hawk dies. I expect the Resistance to keep his promise. I *will* be leader."

She tried not to show her disgust at the notion.

Leadman took Gregan and Tardo with him, heading back to Commspire Oasis to raid its communications gear. Tardo was reluctant to go with Gregan, and Gregan was reluctant to have him. It was only the general's pragmatism, which told him that Tardo was still useful, that stopped Gregan from sending another demon back to Hell.

Taberah made the long trek to Fort Landlock with Mudro and Gouet. There they found the tribes in charge, having routed the Regime forces during Project Trident. The mines were abandoned, and none of the tribespeople had encountered anything remotely like the Birth-masters.

Yet there was one particular passage, in the deepest, darkest parts of the mines, that troubled the tribes to no end. Some disappeared there, and others heard strange noises, and all felt a terrible, evil presence.

"We sealed it up," Sitting Stone told them. "It had bad energy."

"We need to unseal it," Taberah said.

Sitting Stone's eyes widened. "Bad idea."

"Maybe, but we need to walk that tunnel. We need to fight whatever's down there."

Sitting Stone looked at the two Magi. "These are strangers too."

"Welcome strangers," Taberah said.

"They live on many levels."

"I'm happy enough to live on this one," Mudro said, taking a puff of leaf.

"If you open that tunnel, great evil could be released."

Taberah was getting frustrated. "If we don't, great evil can persist."

"We did much work to seal. Many ancient traditions. We came together again, us tribes who so rarely come together, because we all felt evil there. This is evil you do not fight. It is evil you trap."

"For me," Taberah said, "it is evil we kill."

"I will show you way, but will not help you."

"Showing us the way is help enough."

They reached the tunnel, which was sealed up with a giant boulder, into which was carved many symbols, the most prominent of which was a frightening face inside three squares, which Taberah took to mean a prison. Sitting Stone left in a hurry, just as Taberah was taking out some dynamite, and wishing Soasa was there, and having her first doubts about what she was doing—if instead of destroying evil, she was simply freeing it.

Chapter Twenty-five

THE SINS OF SCIENCE

Nissi rushed into the smoke, reaching out for anyone. It was a blind battle and a bare one, a fight of hand and elbow, foot and knee. No one dared fire a bullet on that vessel. Were Rommond alive, even he would not have tried his fabled ricochets, for fear that they might bounce off the bomb.

Nissi grabbed someone in the flurry and the haze, and pulled them to the ground, wrapping her arms around them, and then her legs, adjusting in the struggle until it felt like she had their neck between her knees. It was not a struggle for long then, and her victim's limbs fell limp. The smoke was still thick, so she was not certain of who she had just disarmed, only that it was the enemy.

While Nissi somersaulted around, seizing members of the Armageddon Brigade in choke holds and arm locks, Trokus used brute force, casting fists around in the smog, like he had done for many years in the smog-choked lanes of Rustport, where bare-knuckle boxing was a thing of honour that even the demons abided by. Now he had a reason to punch harder, and endless anger and pain to fuel those strikes.

When the smoke eventually cleared enough to see, there were few people standing, and many lying still, or twitching, on the floor. Nissi and Trokus panted, and turned to face two almost identical men in laboratory coats, both with shoulder-length blonde hair, thick-brimmed glasses, and white gloves holding up flasks of brightly coloured chemicals. Nissi knew them from the early years of the Resistance, when they answered to Rommond. Trokus knew them only from the wanted posters. *The Twisted Twins*. Rommond was blamed for everything they did, whether they answered to him now or not.

"Stay back," the one known as Doctor Elbern said, holding up a green flask. He was the slightly older twin, with the significantly more dour expression, the bully of the brothers.

"Don't come any closer," the one known as Doctor Ekar added with hesitation, after Elbern gave him a vicious elbow. Another stab made him hold up his own vial, containing a bright yellow liquid.

"Don't be fools," Trokus urged. "You'll kill us all."

"No," Elbern said, shaking his head violently, his eyes almost popping from his head. "This isn't real. All of this … is a dream. We'll wake us all up!"

"Then what's stopping you from doing it now?" Nissi asked.

Ekar looked to his brother for the answer.

"It isn't time. It needs to be big. A big bang to wake all the slumbering minds. It's a shared dream, a shared delusion. It's our duty to wake as many as we can."

"You're nuts," Trokus barked.

"No!" Elbern said, holding up a shaking finger. "You're the crazy ones, living in a dream. Rommond almost had us fooled. He's the one pulling the strings, trying to keep us all sleeping."

"Think this through," Nissi urged.

"I already have," the scientist replied. "I've spent most of my life thinking about it. It's time we finally *do* something! This liquid will burn through the floor and burn through the casing of the bomb. Then it will all end."

"Then why are you hesitating?" Nissi asked.

Trokus turned to her, surprised. He did not say it, but his face did: *Stop egging him on*.

Elbern looked to his brother. Ekar looked even less confident than him.

"Are you ready, brother?" Elbern asked.

Ekar made a noticeable gulp. "I'm r—"

At that moment, Armax tumbled through the still open door of the plane, his wings smashing apart on the sides. He stumbled into Elbern, knocking him to the ground, and sending the vial of liquid somersaulting into the air. Nissi snatched it just before it hit the ground. In the confusion, Trokus charged at Ekar, seizing his own corrosive cargo, and pinning him easily against the wall.

"Sorry I'm late," Armax said, kneeling on Elbern's chest. "It's some wind out there."

Nissi smiled. "Perfect timing."

"Where's Jacob?"

"I don't know. Not in here anyway."

"Right then. That must've been him hanging on to the front of the plane all right."

Nissi's eyes widened. "What?"

"I saw someone as I flew past. He's probably mincemeat by now."

Nissi shook her head and grabbed her grappling gun. "Are you two good here?" she asked, before handing Armax the vial.

"We'll be fine," Trokus said. "Go get Jacob."

Nissi nodded, then leapt outside again, firing grappling hooks and swinging to and fro as if it was nothing to her.

"Let us go!" Elbern shouted as Armax continued to press into his ribs. "Why are you helping Rommond? Can't you see that he's the enemy? Can't you see?"

Trokus handed Armax the second vial while he tied Ekar up. The man did not resist, just as he did not resist his brother. Armax waved both vials over Elbern's face, pretending to drop one, forcing the scientist to clench his eyes shut. It was not long before Trokus tied that one up as well.

The hum of the plane was still very loud, and the wind tried to compete with it through the open door. Every so often the vessel shook, and the liquid in the vials shook with it.

"Let's get these out of here," Trokus said.

"Shouldn't we try to disarm the bomb?" Armax asked. He looked towards the sealed door of the cockpit. It would need a bomb of its own to get through.

"The others can do that," Trokus replied. "We need to get the scientists off."

Armax shook his head. "But why?" This was not

Rommond's mission. That was not the instruction the general gave. The scientists did not matter. Their lives did not matter. Only the bomb did.

"If they fail, we need a backup plan," the Regime commander said. "These are the only living people who know how to disarm it."

"Fair enough," Armax said. He limped towards the door, still clutching the two destructive vials, as Trokus brought the prisoners over.

"I don't see your plane," Armax shouted, peering down into the clouds.

"Look closer," Trokus replied, before kicking him out.

Chapter Twenty-six

THE FACILITY

After parting ways with Alex, who decided to go back to the Dune Burrows to see if he could unearth additional antiquities, Brooklyn took the path from Dunedale that was well-known to him, that was programmed into him.

It was a lonely road, the kind unwalked by man and maran. Different feet trod that earth. Metal feet. Brooklyn could not help but find that he was stepping inside the well-formed prints, walking in the footsteps of his iron kin.

Memories stirred in him, but he beat them down, just like he beat the tribesman in the Wild North, just he liked he bashed at Rommond with his gauntlet of metal and wires. He felt a violence in him that was not his own, and yet it owned him.

In time, Brooklyn arrived at what looked like an abandoned test facility, a simple square box, the ultimate expression of Regime architecture. Yet it was a buckled building, with broken windows, through which the dust passed through, like it passed through the Rift. Though it looked deserted, he knew deep down in the very core of him that it was not. It was filled with memories—and other things.

He pressed his hand against the iron door, and felt a shudder inside of him. He had passed through that threshold before, but not willingly. He could feel the burn of the rope around his wrists. He recalled his shouts and pleas, and most especially his cry to Rommond to come and save him. He never came.

He entered the building, where the light barely went. Instinctively, he turned on a flashlight made into his metal limb. He needed to be able to see. He just did not want the mechanical part of him to be his helper. It had never been before.

The upper level was empty, and anyone else would have taken this as proof that the facility was no longer in use. But Brooklyn knew better. He remembered being hauled through those empty rooms, before memory was replaced with a mission. He could almost feel the urge of the mission now. *Target 001.*

He headed down to the second level, which was very different to the first. It was deeper down, but the light was better there. It was artificial light, built by artificial things, to illuminate the artificial. He did not need the flashlight now, but it stayed on.

There were bodies all around the room, on beds and tables, and hanging from the walls. More disturbingly, they were not complete bodies. Torsos were separated from limbs. Heads bobbed in glass jars filled with strange liquids. It was a horrifying sight. It was even more horrifying that Brooklyn recognised it as a memory.

He walked on, trying not to let the sight break his will. He felt an urge to run, and remembered that feeling from before, when he was strapped down and filled with paralysing drugs, before he was taken apart, all while he was still awake, and still aware. He had seen parts of him being taken away, and foreign parts put in their place. He had been forced to watch them change him, unable to do anything to stop the process.

He passed by large tanks of black liquid, and though he could see nothing there, he could hear the movement inside. There were buried memories of that too, of the submersion, of the days and days of feeling that he was drowning, and the nights of blindness, and the never sleeping, and the never blinking, and the barely breathing through tubes and wires.

It took a great struggle to continue on, and not simply take a blade to his neck or a bullet to his head. Yet he knew with grim certainty that he would not die there. They would take his corpse and make it living again. Though there would be only a fraction of him left by the time they were through with him, that fraction would be conscious of all the changes, and unable to do anything to stop it.

He was made in that room, but it did not feel like it was home. It was a temporary prison, where they worked on the more permanent prison of his body. He had to find the jailer, and had to get the key.

He continued through until he came to a door down to the next level. He knew he had been down there too, but the memory was very faint. He was fully one of the Iron Guard then, under the iron grip of the Controller. He pushed the door open, vowing never to be controlled again.

Chapter Twenty-seven

FREEFALL

R ommond struggled with the burning remains of his plane as it spiralled swiftly to the ground. It spun so quickly that his mind spun too, and his eyes found it difficult to focus on the rotating sky around him, which was becoming a sky of fire by the minute.

He felt the heat approaching, and growing, as the fire ate away at the wooden panels and melted the metal ones. He knew he had to get out quick, but did not want to break his back in the process. He considered opening the canopy and leaping off the edge, manually opening his parachute, but he feared the flames would eat that too.

You need to live, he thought, reconciling himself with the idea of spending his remaining days shackled to a chair, wheeled about by Brooklyn, if the tribesman even returned from the east. He was gone five years the last time he was dragged there. It was madness that he now went there willingly. Rommond only hoped he found find what he was looking for.

You need to live for him, the general told himself.

He pulled the lever between his legs, and heard a click. He closed his eyes and waited for the force of the springs. Then nothing happened. He opened his eyes, and saw the burning shell still around him. Then he yanked the handle again, much more forcefully, and he heard several more clicks, but still he sat in the plummeting wreckage, growing dizzier by the second.

"Damn it."

He stretched his boot towards the backpack on the floor, which slid from side to side as the vessel continued to drop. He caught one of the straps around his toes and tugged it towards him, before grabbing it and hugging it close. He felt the straps of the seat holding him in place, stopping him from bashing off the dashboard or the glass. He knew he would have to free himself from those restraints. This was Plan B, and it was not a good one. His mind did not come up with it; his instincts did. He had to time it well or he risked being flung out in the downward spin, and breaking more than just his back. He needed to jump, not be thrown, to avoid the falling hull striking him on his way down, or his parachute getting entangled in it, or the fire leaping out to burn a hole in the fabric.

He knew he would never be able to get the backpack on his back without first unbuckling himself, which would then see him thrown around the cockpit like a rag doll. He settled on putting it on backwards, over his chest, where he could still get the straps on, and would be able to clutch the pack as he fell.

With the backpack in place, he reached for the gas mask dangling from the dashboard, and quickly pulled it over his face. There was some oxygen in its chambers, but he feared there was not enough. There was precious little this high up, and the fire was using that up swiftly.

He pushed open the canopy shell, and even with the gas mask, he almost choked on the fumes. Black smoke swarmed him, and orange embers scalded any part of him that was exposed.

He braced his right foot against the edge of the cockpit wall, then unbuckled his restraints, and jumped over the side, piercing the cloud of smoke. The flames seized him and set his uniform alight, but his swift descent extinguished them. That was the only time he was thankful for the fall.

He tumbled, and the plane tumbled with him. He had not managed to jump far enough away, or maybe he did, and the wind brought him back close to the wreckage, like fate ushering him towards his coffin.

He tried to regain control of his fall, but the sky continued to toss him, so that at every fraction of a second he saw the alternation of the ground and sky. His brain felt like it was expanding in his head. He felt weak. He could not see properly. It was all a burning blur. He felt himself fading out of consciousness, and for a moment it all went black, and it was kind of peaceful, until the sounds blared suddenly, and the sights stabbed his aching eyes.

He kicked his legs, but continued to tumble. He kicked again, and again, until finally he kicked against the hull of the monoplane, and managed to simultaneously right himself and push himself away.

He reached about his body, but was so dis-orientated he was not sure where he was reaching. *String*, he thought, but the thought was a struggle. He felt about for something to pull, but could not feel anything, and could not see anything. Even the gas mask conspired against him, blocking his vision.

Then he grabbed it, and yanked it hard. He heard a flutter of fabric, then felt a harsh tug upwards as the wind hauled the parachute up. He let out a long sigh, and felt he had time now to attend to the overwhelming feeling of nausea.

But he was still dropping fast, faster than he should have been if the parachute was working. He heard a whistle of wind, and glanced up to see a large hole in the canopy above, through which the air rushed through. He knew with grim certainty that the parachute would not ease his fall, and if he did not know it then, he would have learned it from the quickly-approaching ground, with not a cushioning area in sight.

What false hope, he thought, shaking his head. He had been a fool to trust in it. He knew better. Hope was the enemy.

Chapter Twenty-eight

SORRY

Whistler saw the Regime planes turning, and spotted Trokus bundling the scientists on board his own. The canopy closed shut, and then the commander turned as well to flee the scene.

"What's going on?" the boy called into the radio. "Why are you leaving?"

"We got what we came for," Trokus replied.

"But ... the bomb?"

"I don't think there's any stopping that now."

"But surely we have to try."

"Go home, boy. It's over."

Whistler had been born into the Resistance. He knew that while any of them yet lived, it was not over. The fight continued. He was not of fighting age, but he had to fight all the same.

He turned his plane and pursued the Regime vessels. He knew in his heart that they had betrayed the mission. Rommond would never have let the scientists get out alive. If they were taken by the Regime, the Iron Emperor would make many more of those world-destroying bombs. Maybe Altadas would not be the only world where he dropped them.

"Turn back, boy," Trokus warned.

"I can't. I can't let you do this."

"I have to. I don't want to, but I have to."

"Then I have to stop you."

"Turn back. You don't have to die for this."

Whistler did not reply. He gained on them, which was response enough.

"Fine," Trokus said with a sigh. "Shoot him down."

The three Regime monoplanes turned sharply, and the gun barrels locked into place. Whistler spun his plane to avoid the initial barrage of bullets, then had to drop quickly to dodge the next. The enemy vessels split apart, then came at him from every angle. He had to use every trick he knew, and invent new ones, to get out of the line of fire, and no matter how hard he tried, the hull of his aircraft was peppered with holes.

He pulled up sharply, and kept pulling, until he turned full circle and ended up behind the nearest plane. He closed his eyes and gripped the trigger, hearing the iron rattle, followed by an explosion outside. Then he heard the screams of the pilot over the radio, and wished he could turn it off.

"I'm sorry," Whistler sobbed.

He did not want to have to stay it two more times.

The remaining fighters split apart and came at him again, and Whistler rolled and dodged. One of them entered his field of fire, but his hand resisted the trigger, and he chose to veer off to the side instead. He flew into the cover of the clouds, circling in place.

"I can't do this," he said to himself. "I'm not a fighter."

After circling several more times, he came out of the cloud on the other side, and spotted the quickly-disappearing aircraft further ahead. He could try to chase them, but he knew it would be difficult to catch up, and even more difficult to find the cold-hearted killer in him to bring them down.

"I'm sorry, Rommond," he said, and when he thought of the bigger picture, he added: "I'm sorry, world."

Chapter Twenty-nine

UNDER CONTROL

Brooklyn continued down deeper into the facility, finding himself in a part unlike the rest. It was much older, with moss-covered brick, and a stone altar illuminated by light streaming in from a circular hole in the ceiling.

It was there that he found her.

The Controller.

She stood in the spotlight, the light glinting off the silver edges of her iron armour, highlighting all the interlocking pieces, all the squares and diamonds, and shapes that did not have a name.

"You use temple," Brooklyn said disapprovingly.

"It is just brick and mortar," she replied. "No gods dwell here now."

"You are wrong. I feel them now."

It was hard to tell if she smiled at him from beneath her mask. "Then call me faithless. I believe only in iron, and the god who gave it to us: the Iron Emperor."

"He is no god. He is man."

"No," she said, shaking her head. "He is not a man. He is so much more."

"Then call me faithless," Brooklyn replied. It was

difficult for him to mock her, when he tried to find the good in all, but it was difficult to see the good in her.

"You cannot be faithless, when you're so zealous," the Controller said, flicking a switch on her belt.

Brooklyn felt his will immediately suppressed. Another power stood upon it, pulling the strings. He lost complete control of his ability to move. He was just a passenger in his own body.

"Now bow," she said, pressing another button.

Brooklyn bowed low.

"Now kneel."

He got down on his knees.

"Now pray."

He pressed his hands and forehead against the ground, and whispered something in the maran tongue.

Then she let him go, and he got back to his feet, exhausted from the inner struggle.

"See," she said. "You cannot be faithless when you pray to the Iron Emperor."

Brooklyn gulped hard, and clenched his fists. "You can make my body move, but not my soul. It is soul that prays. All else is passing."

"Give me time, Brooklyn," she said, "and I will dig deep enough to find your soul. I will find a way to make it kneel as well."

Brooklyn heard familiar whispers. "The spirits are angry."

"There are no spirits, Brooklyn. You have deluded yourself. There is only your body, my puppet, and your wires, my strings."

It was then that he saw the other figures emerging from the darkness, all those other puppets answering her call. The Iron Guard stood forth, aiming their iron eyes at him, and their iron limbs, with their iron guns.

"Come," the Controller said, "sit on the shelves with your brothers and sisters. Add yourself to my collection. I have so few ... tribal dolls."

Brooklyn glared at her. "No."

She flicked the switch, and he stepped forward involuntarily. She flicked it back, and he stepped back.

"Why refuse? What does it accomplish?"

"I am not your slave."

She smiled, and flicked the switch again. "But you are."

He lurched forward, his limbs seizing up, the fluidity replaced by the harsh and awkward movement of something mechanical. She let him go again so he could speak of his own accord.

"Why fight?" she asked him.

"Because freedom is worth fighting for."

"Is it? Whose words are those you're parroting? Isn't that just a form of mental slavery? You fight for the so-called Resistance, and yet you do everything they say. You follow their rules, their code. You speak their words and spread their propaganda. You fight and die for a cause, because a cause gives meaning to your otherwise meaningless lives. You've always been a slave. You're a slave to your instincts. You're a slave to biology. You're a slave to nature. Maybe it's comforting to tug on the strings, but it's also comforting to just let go."

"Perhaps you're right," Brooklyn said, "but easy road is rarely right road. We struggle for bigger things. What you do is wrong. That is why we must fight you."

He pressed forward towards her, but she flicked the switch as he neared, and he stopped suddenly.

She smiled. "You fight if I let you fight."

Then she paused suddenly as she heard a click. She looked to her belt, where the switch had moved back to the off position.

Brooklyn looked at her, with his own eyes. He stepped forward.

"Just a malfunction," the Controller said, striking the switch again.

Brooklyn halted and straightened up. The iron in him was stronger than his muscles.

Then they heard the click again, and he was back.

The mask hid her shock, but the Controller backed away.

"Do you not feel in control?" Brooklyn asked her.

"It's *just* a malfunction," she insisted.

"Once, error. Twice, thing of note. Three times, work of something higher."

She forced the switch back on, but it immediately turned off, and despite all her efforts to move it, it seemed to be jammed.

"I don't understand," she said.

"The machine spirits are everywhere, and because you put machinery in me, and machinery on you, they are in me and on you too."

"But I don't believe—"

"You don't have to believe. You will know."

The oil lamps flickered low, and the shadows deepened.

The Controller looked to either side of her, where the Iron Guard stood still. She issued commands to all of them, and they started to advance towards Brooklyn.

Yet, as some of them passed by the experiment tables, where mechanical limbs were arranged for surgical replacement of human or maran ones, those limbs came suddenly to life, and reached out to the advancing mechanical men.

Everything that was metal or wire came to life in the temple, and moved towards the Iron Guard to block their way. Bars flew like projectiles, and crates barred like mines.

"So you have your own Iron Guard," the Controller said.

Brooklyn smiled at her. "I have yours as well."

Every switch on her belt flicked off, and the Iron Guard stood still. The red in their eyes faded, and they glanced around the room, and at each other, in bewilderment. Their movements were less mechanical, and when they looked upon the Controller, their anger was real.

"I made you," she told them as they advanced on her.

Brooklyn turned away as they grabbed her, tearing off the silver-edged iron plates of her armour, breaking apart the mask that hid her burnt and disfigured face, the product of the Iron Plague. She was a thin and frail figure beneath the armour, slowly crumbling apart.

The Iron Guard had lost many years of their lives to her puppetry. Some lost close to a decade. Many lost limbs. Some lost eyes. They suffered torture and misery at her hands, and at the hands of the doctors and surgeons of Project Ironbreath. For all those lost days, they were still there, buried beneath the weight of wires, imprisoned in their own bodies. They knew very well that she made them, and that is why they were driven by an uncontrollable rage to unmake her.

Chapter Thirty

A LITTLE BIT OF CRAZY

As Jacob clung to the windscreen, waiting and praying for help, he saw Cala's smiling face inside. She waved at him in an animated way. Though he could not hear her, he could see her mouthing words at him, which looked a little like, "Wave back, honey. Don't you know it's rude not to wave?" She turned to her co-pilots, and mouthed, "We used to date, me and him. Isn't he handsome?"

Just when Jacob almost felt like letting go, a firm hand gripped his wrist, and Nissi hauled him back up. Cala's shock was evident, and she kicked the windscreen with her boots.

"Not a great idea to block the pilots' view," Nissi told him.

"I'm not known for my great ideas."

He held onto her as she fired grappling hooks left and right, swinging across like the queen of the aerial jungle.

"You make it look so easy," Jacob told her. He was glad it was easy for her, or he might still be clutching the windscreen.

The compliment had little effect on Nissi's composure. "When you've done tightrope walking between two hot air balloons at twenty thousand feet, it becomes second nature."

"Bit of a thrill-seeker, eh?"

"You could say that."

"Well, I've just seen an old thrill-seeker blast from the past in the cockpit."

"Can't wait to meet him."

"Her, and I think *I* can wait."

They swung for a moment, back and forth, as Nissi tried to usher them closer to the door.

"Cosy," Jacob said, hanging on tight.

"You sure you're not uncomfortable being rescued by a woman?"

"No. I could get used to it."

"With your poor balance, seems like you might have to."

"Ouch."

They swung inside, and Nissi rolled on the floor, while Jacob fell face-first. They barely had time enough to feel solid ground beneath them before they saw Cala standing there, swinging a crowbar in Nissi's direction.

"Come on!" she roared.

Nissi looked to Jacob. "Is this who you were on about?"

Cala's eyes widened. "You were talking about me?" She swung the crowbar a little more wildly, and Nissi backed away. "What were you saying?" she asked, shifting from manic smiles to intense frowns. "Huh?"

"Cala, put the crowbar down," Jacob said.

"But I've gotta defend myself," she replied. "There

are people, like her, coming to get me. I'm one of the few who've woken up, y'know, and that makes me a threat. They want to smother me with a pillow. They want to send me back to sleep. But I'm keeping my eyes *wide* open!" She pulled the eyelids of her left eye as wide apart as she could, as if she was about to use a hallucinogenic eyebox.

"What if you're wrong?" Jacob asked. "What if it's these people you're with now, this Armageddon Brigade, that has you dreaming. What if they don't want you to wake up to the reality that they're just psychopaths?"

"I'm not a fool," Cala said, shaking her head so forcefully that some of her hair came loose from its bobbin. "I'd know if I was being conned."

While Jacob spoke, Nissi attempted to sneak up on Cala, but Cala noticed, and threw the crowbar at her. It struck Nissi's arm as she guarded her face from the projectile.

"Stay back, sleepwalker!" Cala shouted.

She raced towards her, but Nissi unleashed one of her grappling hooks, firing the metal claw straight into Cala's face. They could hear the crunch, right before her dreadful scream.

Cala fell to the ground, clutching her bloodied face. "My nose!" she cried. "You broke my nose!" She rolled about for a bit, shouting and grunting, then started laughing loudly, snorting on the blood as she cackled.

"Crikey," Nissi said. "What is *wrong* with her?"

Cala sat up and pointed to her buckled nose. "Isn't it obvious?"

Nissi was caught off guard as Cala suddenly spit blood into her eyes. She lunged at her and tried to claw at her face, then bashed her head against the ground until she passed out. She would have kept bashing and clawing had Jacob not grabbed her and pulled her away.

"It's a mask she's wearing," Cala said, struggling with Jacob, "all prettied up for the boys. She's ugly underneath. Let me show you!"

"Stop this, Cala!" Jacob urged. "We didn't come here to fight you."

"I know," she said, pawing his face with her blood-covered fingers. "I know you came for me."

He recoiled from her, and she became more violent, slapping him.

"What is it?" she pleaded. "Is it her? Huh? Old red-head? What do you see in her? She's nothing. She's no fun. Oh, *yes*, she runs the fabled Order. Hell, she *is* Order. But *I'm* Chaos, and Chaos is a lot more fun, Jakey boy, a lot more! You know that. You know that deep down, down where it counts." She grinned and ground her body against his. "You can paint yourself up real good, but you're still scum like the rest of us. You ain't no soldier boy, Jake. The uniform's all illusion." She held her hands out. "It's all a dream."

"It's just like you to buy into that," Jacob said. "You volunteered to work at the nut house."

"I know they're crazy," Cala said, rotating her index finger at her temple. "That's why I'm here. Not because *I'm* crazy. No, Jakey boy, don't give me that look! They're just ... a lot more fun. A lot more fun than you so-called 'normal' people." She indicated the quotation marks with her fingers.

She drew up close, close enough that he could feel her hot breath upon his skin—almost close enough that he could hear her thoughts. "They think this is all a dream, and I kind of like that idea. Y'see, then we can change it into anything we want. It's all formless. It's all fluid."

"Then why try to destroy it?" Jacob asked.

She shrugged. "Maybe I never planned to drop the bomb. Or maybe I just wanted to see what'd happen. Don't you like the idea of being able to change the entire world in an instant? I have that power right now. They made me God." She tapped her fingers off her chest, her eyes wide with the wonder of it all. "They made me God."

"Then have mercy on these people."

"Mercy? No ... not that God. They made me the Destroyer."

"And what will you accomplish with that?"

She shrugged again. "I don't know. And that's the fun of it. But still ... it got your attention, didn't it? After all those years of ignoring me, here you are. This time you came to *me*. I didn't have to go chasing you, Jake. You're the one who came running."

"But not for you," he said, and regretted saying it. He realised he probably should have been appeasing her, not making her angry.

"You're a liar," she said. "I know, 'cause ... you're, you're just a liar. You sensed I was here. I know you did. We've ... we've got a connection. You can't deny that, Jakey boy. You can't hide what you feel."

Like pity? he thought.

"You can run away from me," she continued, "but you can't run away from *us*."

There's no us, he thought. *There never was.* He could not understand why she did not see that. When they met, they had so many holes, they tried to fill them with thrills. But the thrills kept falling through, so they needed bigger ones to plug the gaps. But the holes grew larger as well. Maybe love could seal them up for good, but he never felt that with her, and he did not think she felt it either. He was just another addiction, an obsession, one she seemed unable to shake. Maybe the Worldwaker was the cure.

Chapter Thirty-one

A FABULOUS COPTER

Rommond had resigned himself to his fate, letting the wind whip him, letting it beat at his eardrums until all other sounds were muted. And yet, there was another sound, and it was not his breath, or his heart, or the hiss of smoke, or the crackle of fire, or the whistle of wind. It was mechanical.

The clouds did not so much as part, but were parted, and what dispersed them was a sight to behold: an odd amalgamation of machinery, with wheels and wings, treads and balloons, and many rotating propellers to match its many bulbous windows. It was a haphazard design, if it could even be called *designed*, and it was cobbled together as though its owner had not decided if he wanted it to swim or sail, or float or fly, or just crawl across the desert sand.

It made a tremendous din, with all those rotating parts. It was not just the sound of movement, but the sound of things momentarily breaking down and starting up again. This constant to and fro, stopping and starting, meant the vessel did not really hover, but fell and rose again.

Rommond merely fell, but the strange copter followed him, dropping sharply, then sending up a plume of steam and smoke as the engines kicked in again. He saw a shaft open, and a large mechanical arm reached out. It grabbed him in its pincers, and the pinch was painful. But Rommond was glad to feel pain, because for a moment there it seemed like he was never going to feel anything again.

He was pulled inside, and the hatch slammed shut. While his eyes adjusted slowly to the darkness, he heard the pumping of many pistons, the clank of shifting cogs, the whistle of steam escaping through metal flumes, and a constant clang of metal, the music of a smithy. His head still spun, and his eyes still stung, but he could now see the globular chamber he lay in, and the metal scraps and junk around and beneath him.

A door inside the vessel swung open, and a dim light poured in. In the threshold stood a familiar silhouette, tall and thin, with the most oversized hat ever known to man or woman.

"Porridge," Rommond said with a smile.

Porridge stepped forward, the heels of his pointed leopardskin shoes adding to the percussion of the ship's engineering. He wore a long yellow coat, skin-tight purple trousers, and a blouse of rose-coloured frills. The hat was made of many feathers and many hues, like a peacock's tail, or perhaps even the real thing.

"Oh!" Porridge cried, in as high a pitch as possible. "My dear boy! Oh! What've they done to you, sweetie?" He rushed over, swinging his arms, prancing over the debris inside the room. He tried to haul Rommond up, but did not have much strength for that. Rommond had to give what little he had left to clamber to his feet.

"I'm okay," the general said, but he knew he was not. The fall had taken a lot out of him. The landing would have taken the rest.

"Let's get you to my quarters, plum," Porridge said, as Rommond leant heavily upon him. His already rosy cheeks flushed crimson. "Oh! My spinning cogs! To think they could've killed you!" He almost fainted at the notion, which would not have done much good for his efforts to support Rommond.

"It's lucky you were here," the general said, each word a labour to pronounce.

Porridge stumbled with Rommond towards the door, his hat falling off to reveal his golden-brown curls. He leant against the frame for a moment and shouted down the corridor, where several oil lamps threw out a faint glimmer.

"Bitnickle!" he cried.

A clockwork contraption rolled down the corridor on one large wheel, at the front, and one smaller wheel at the back. It had a thin metal frame emerging from the larger wheel, with two mechanical arms extending from this, bearing the same kind of pincer claws that Porridge used to haul Rommond inside. The creature had a large torch light for a head, which shone brightly upon the duo now. A radio strapped to its torso turned on and off periodically, the dial rotating seemingly of its own accord, allowing it to speak with snippets of Regime broadcasting.

"What is it … Emperor?" the clockwork being asked, switching between a feature on what motivates the evil General Rommond, and a news report on the attendance of the Iron Emperor at the Iron Rally.

"Oh, isn't she a sweetheart?" Porridge said. "Can you get a glass of water for our guest?"

"... certainly ..." The radio was speaking about the many psychological defects of those attracted to the Resistance movement, with one "expert" stating that they *certainly* showed all the signs of madness. He recommended heavy dosing, permanent restraints, and constant supervision.

Bitnickle rolled off, and returned just as swiftly, clutching a half-spilled glass of water. Porridge handed it to Rommond as they sat with their backs against the frame of the door.

"Didn't think the Clockwork Commune were this friendly," the general commented after gulping down the fluid. He needed a drink, but water was not what he had in mind.

Bitnickle hung her lamp-shaped head, shining a spotlight on the oil-stained floor. The stench of oil was thick, but the smell of Porridge's perfume was thicker.

"She's one of the good ones," Porridge said, and Bitnickle's head rose again. "Got her from the Coilhunter. He's got one of his own up there in the Wild North."

"Sometimes I wish I had his job," Rommond said.

Porridge giggled. "And I bet he wishes he had yours, cupcake."

"How did you know I was here?"

"I didn't. I was following that wingship with the bomb for a while, keeping a safe distance. I thought the design looked familiar, but then people've been stealing dear Brooklyn's blueprints for ages now. Oh! My shock when I realised it was you in one of the other wingships! And bless my crumbling heart when I saw you go down. I thought I'd never make it down in time!" He placed the back of his hand against his forehead, and unearthed a multicoloured fan with his other hand to cool himself down.

"I probably don't say this often enough, my dear chap," Rommond said, "but thank you."

"Oh, it's nothing, really, my dearest dandy. I'm just glad I was there to save the day! Oh, you'll be doing a painting of me now and hanging it in your quarters, won't you, sweetie? Hero of the hour! Who'd have thought, poor delicate flower like me?"

Rommond smiled. "We're all full of surprises. But maybe you can be hero of a lifetime. There's still a bomb out there in the clouds, and I need your help to stop it going off."

Chapter Thirty-two

ENDING EVERYTHING

Rommond joined Porridge in the cockpit of his strange copter, which was perhaps still less strange than its driver, who had dubbed the vessel the Dandyman. The whirling blades spun faster, and the vessel ascended into the clouds, exuding enough smoke and steam to add some clouds of its own.

"Bring us over the cockpit if you can," Rommond ordered. Perhaps he should have been requesting, asking nicely, or even begging, but he was too used to giving orders, and Porridge was the kind of man who liked to pretend he was submissive.

"Oooh!" he cried, blushing. "Tell me where to park it, plum."

Rommond pointed as he talked. "If you can get me close enough to the hatch on the roof, and maybe put that lever arm of yours into business, I can sort out the pilots inside."

"I can land *on* the wingship, and clamp on tight," Porridge said. "And I'll have that hatch door off before you can say 'butter me for breakfast'!"

He flew the copter over the Dreamdevil, matching its speed with ease, then descended suddenly, striking the roof of the aeroplane with a screech. Clamps extended from the vessel and latched on tight.

"Oh, do forgive me, daisy!" Porridge said. "It's always a hard landing."

Rommond hurried out onto the roof just as Porridge was tearing off the hatch door with his vessel's mechanical arm.

The general jumped down into the cockpit, and was immediately confronted by one of the pilots, who knocked Rommond's pistol from his hand. Had he not being weakened by his tumble from the heavens, he would have easily overpowered the pilot, but his muscles were fatigued. They struggled, pushing and pulling, shimmying around the small control room like aggressive dancers.

The other pilot stayed at his post, but was forced to flinch and duck as the struggle came his way. Rommond shoved his attacker against the controls, and switches were flipped, and dials spun. Then the vessel nose-dived suddenly, and all three of them fell against the windscreen with a thud. Even from that position they could hear the bomb outside striking the underside of the plane, and the nerve-racking groaning of the cables that held it in place.

The fight was abandoned momentarily as all three men clambered up and tried to right the plane. It was a frantic bashing of buttons as gravity pulled them towards the window, and the plane towards the ground.

"What's going on down there?" Porridge called down through the shaft, popping his head through.

The pilots steadied the craft, and the nose swung up suddenly. Porridge tumbled down into the room with a cry, a tangle of lanky limbs and gaudy coat tails.

The fight started anew, but this time both pilots charged at Rommond. Porridge was dusting himself off when he too was caught in the fray. He shrieked as he was tossed back and forth between the assailants like a weapon.

"I'm neutral!" he yelled, before elbowing one of the pilots in the eye.

The distraction was enough for Rommond to overpower the other pilot and slam his face against one of the steel chairs, knocking him out cold. He was the lucky one, because Rommond dived for his pistol, turned sharply, and took the other pilot out with hot metal.

Porridge shuddered as the pilot slumped to the ground near his feet. He grabbed the chair for support, and whipped out his fan. "Oh, Rommond, I could never do what you do, buttercup!" He saw splatters of blood on his gown, like new crimson polka dots "Look at my outfit!"

"I need you to do something else," Rommond said. "Can you fly this?"

"Oh, I don't know. There are a lot of doodahs to pull, but I think I'll manage, darling."

"Put us on a course as far away from populated regions as possible … just in case."

"Oh, Rommond! Don't say that!"

"I have to, because this isn't over yet."

He pulled at the door leading to the rest of the plane, but it was jammed. He could hear the rattle of a crowbar on the other side, and a female voice shouting at Jacob.

* * *

Cala took another hit of Hope. "That's the stuff. Oh, it really gets you. There's no hiding from it. It knows where you are. It knows how to bring you out. You look like you need that, Jakey boy. You look like you need someone to find you. I know you're in there, deep inside, still the same Jake I knew. You're in there somewhere. Come and have a sniff. It'll do you wonders!"

He knocked the bag from her hand, and the dust went everywhere.

"Are you mad?" she cried. "That stuff costs a fortune!"

"Not that you pay for it."

She thrust her hips, and the tight brown leather creaked. "I pay for it just fine."

She knocked him to the floor, clawing and screaming. "Your eyes clean, Jake?" She pulled down her own goggles, then produced an eyebox from her belt, two little cubes attached to a pair of goggles. She pressed them against Jacob's eyes.

For a moment, he was stunned, and he stopped resisting her. His eyes were enraptured by the sight in the eyebox. It was like looking at the universe, a hundred thousand million stars, all swirling, all making him dizzy, all pulling him in, hypnotising him.

He bashed the box away, and it took all his strength to do it.

"No!" Cala cried, clambering off him and holding up the broken eyebox. "You're ruining it all! You're ruining all the fun!"

"This *isn't* a game!"

"It is. Everything is."

"Well, then you lost," Jacob said, standing up. "We control this plane now. Rommond's in there. We're going to land this thing, and we're going to disarm the bomb. It's over, Cala. Just ... give up."

Cala shook her head. "No. You clearly don't understand. It doesn't end like this. It can't! It *has* to be like fireworks. Don't you see, Jake? Don't you see?"

Jacob sighed. "No, Cala. I don't. I don't think I ever did. I just ... don't see things like you do. This isn't a game to me. This is real. And I want it to keep being real. When I was with you, we were living a dream ... a fantasy. I've found people I can be myself with. I found a place where I fit in."

"That's the dream, Jake," she told him through her tears and the tangle of her unkempt hair. "There's no such thing as a perfect family. There's no such thing as a happy ending. You might think the candle's still burning bright, Jakey boy, but sooner or later all our lights go out. And it can fizzle, and send up a tiny stream of smoke, or it can all be brash and blinding. Life's boring enough as it is. Why be boring too?"

Jacob shrugged ever so slightly. "I guess because it makes me happy. What's all this excitement ever done for you?"

She gave a fierce frown, and struggled with her emotions. "You're trying to trick me!" She said it more to herself than him. "I can't believe it! Not you! Not you, Jakey boy. *Anyone* but you. I've tried to help you! But you're trying to get inside my head. You're playing mind games with me! Oh, no! You get out now!" She pawed her head. "You had your chance. You blew it. And now I'm gonna blow it too."

She grabbed the crowbar that held the cockpit door shut, and then threw herself outside, with not a hint of concern for where she might land. She struck the bomb with a clang, and caught one of the wires holding it in place. Immediately she started banging the weapon with the tool in her hand, whacking it until there were dents in the metal.

"Stop!" Jacob shouted down to her. "You've got to stop this!"

"I'm stopping it!" she yelled back up. "I'm stopping it all!"

Rommond stumbled into the room, ready for a fight, but found Jacob standing there, and Nissi lying there unconscious amidst a pile of other bodies.

"That woman," Rommond said. "Where is she?"

"Eh ... out there." Jacob pointed to the open door.

Rommond bowed his head slightly. "It's probably for the best."

"No, I mean ... she's still alive. She's on the bomb."

"She's what?" Rommond charged over to the door and looked down to where Cala was sitting with the bomb between her legs like a horse. "God," he said.

"He ain't listening, sweet-cheeks," Cala shouted up. "And I've been praying real hard." She gave the bomb a few more whacks. "Hey, can you do me a favour and throw me down some tools? This isn't quite doing the trick."

Rommond turned to Jacob. "We need to stop

her."

"Yeah, I kind of gathered that."

Rommond took out his pistol and held it up.

"What if you miss?" Jacob asked.

"We probably won't live long enough to regret it."

Jacob pursed his lips. "How many bullets have you got?"

"It doesn't matter," Rommond replied. "I only need one."

He went back to the doorway and leant against the edge.

"There you are!" Cala shouted up. "Where's my tools?"

He pointed the pistol at her and tried to steady his hands. The movement of the plane did not help, nor did her swaying from the wires. She rode the bomb like a swing. She looked up at him and smiled.

"Go ahead," she said. "Blow a hole in it."

He fired, and the bullet struck its mark, piercing her forehead. The look of shock on her face was frightening, and yet no more frightening than the manic expression she often had. There was a smile in that shock, like she somehow enjoyed it, like she found it all exciting. The blood ran down her face, and she collapsed.

Her bloodied body slumped off the edge, and fell into the depths below. Yet even in her final descent, it almost seemed like she had a sliver of a smile. It had been fun while it lasted. Death was just another adventure. Jacob hoped she would not haunt him from the afterlife.

"It's done," Rommond said, patting Jacob on the

shoulder. It was a reassuring pat, as if he recognised that part of Jacob felt a loss, that, as crazy as she was, the smuggler had had some sympathy for her.

"Yeah," Jacob said, with a sigh. "I guess it's really over."

They turned away from the open door, relaxing their shoulders, taking easier breaths than they had taken before, only to be startled by the sound of snapping wires as the Worldwaker loosened from its bonds.

Chapter Thirty-three

THREAD

Rommond charged back into the control room, barely stopping for breath.

"Your copter," he said, panting. "You need to fly it under the bomb."

"*Under* the bomb?" Porridge asked with incredulity.

"It's breaking! It's falling!"

The general dragged the trader from his seat, tripping over the bodies of the pilots.

"You need to get under there," he urged. "You need to support it."

Porridge panicked, waving his hands about frantically. "Oh, Rommond, dearie, that's too much responsibility for me. What if I don't succeed?"

Rommond cut even his own sigh short. "Never mind," he said, as he belted up the ladder to the copter, shouting for Jacob as he went.

Jacob entered the cockpit to find Porridge pointing up the ladder. "Oh, do be careful! That's my livelihood up there."

Jacob raised an eyebrow. "That's all our livelihoods below us."

He joined Rommond in the cockpit of the copter,

and barely sat down before the general issued a bullet list of orders. "Get some coal in that engine. I need lift. You'll have to control the arm. I can barely fly this thing."

Jacob followed the commands as best he could, starting by shovelling several scoops of coal into the burner. He toiled away until his hands were black, and the flames spat at him, disrespecting the man that fed them.

"That's enough," Rommond barked. "Get those pistons going." He pointed to the pumps near the burner, painted in different bright colours for what seemed like purely aesthetic reasons.

"How?" Jacob asked.

"The lever!"

He noticed the lever on the side of the pumps, and pulled it down hard. It resisted his force, and sprang up again. The pistons rose and fell a few times, then slowed to a stop.

"It's not working," he said.

"Keep at it! You need to crank it more than once."

Jacob tried again, pulling harshly, then letting the spring set it back into place, before tugging it down again. The pumps got faster, but it still did not seem like they could be left to their own accord. He cranked the lever several more times, getting a feel for the biting point when he had to crank it again before it returned fully to its neutral position. He heard the hum of the pistons, and saw the sizzle of steam, but most of all he felt the vessel raising up off the Dreamdevil beneath.

Rommond flew the copter forward, and it was

an unsteady movement. The propellers spun at phenomenal speeds, until the blades could no longer be seen. At the mere press of a button, a hatch would open somewhere on the vessel, and another, smaller propeller would pop out and start spinning, pushing the craft in the opposite direction. It took much trial and error—and there was a lot of error—for the general to figure out which button did what. One of the propellers ground off the windscreen of the Dreamdevil, and Jacob could see Porridge almost fainting inside.

Another wire snapped, and the bomb swung forward, with just two more cables keeping it in place. The weight of the weapon swung towards the copter.

"Watch out!" Jacob cried, as if Rommond could not see it.

It was too late. The bomb struck the copter with a bang, and sent it spinning away. Rommond quickly regained control, though now several of the propeller blades were bent, and the copter had less thrust, and he had less control.

Jacob shook his head. *We're not going to make it*, he thought, as he saw the bomb hanging by its two final threads. They might have been big threads, thick threads, but there were still just two of them. They were all that stood between the world and annihilation.

As he grimaced at the groaning of the wires, he heard a sudden whoosh of air and thrum of an engine. He looked out and was glad to see a monoplane whiz by, and even gladder to see the number on its tail fin.

"Whistler!" Jacob cried.

"Get his frequency," Rommond ordered, nudging the nearby radio. It was set to a different channel than what Trokus set up for them on the other planes.

Jacob messed with the dials. "Damn it, I can't remember."

"Well, you better hope he's psychic then."

Chapter Thirty-four

THE BATTLE OF
THE BIRTH-MASTERS

The explosion ripped through the tunnels of Fort Landlock, and the barrier was broken. Taberah felt it coming down, and she knew the Magi felt it too.

"I suppose we have no choice now," Mudro said.

Taberah hauled up her weapons bag. "No."

"You better hope we end this."

"One way or another, this ends for us."

They followed the winding path down until it opened into an immense chamber, a cavern leading out into many smaller caverns. It almost looked like the womb of the world. Across its surface were hundreds of Glass crystals, of all shapes and sizes, and different shades of white or blue, or completely translucent, or a mix of the two. They rose from the ground, and jutted out of the walls, and hung from the ceiling. If this was a womb, then they were the placenta, nourishing and protecting the chamber. Yet they almost looked like a set of teeth as well. It was less inspiring to think that they stood inside a mouth.

The Birth-masters stood upon a dais in the darkness, taller than most marans, and illuminated only by the faint glimmer that came from the Glass.

The cast great shadows on the orange walls, the kind of shadows that did not match up to their bodies. They looked a lot more demonic, bent out of shape, with large claws, and larger horns. The shadows continued to twist and contort, even when the men stood still, and even when the light did not shift.

They wore long, hooded robes, each a different colour. The closest wore blue, while the two at the back wore red and yellow. All three carried long staffs of gnarled wood.

They stood in a perfect triangle, in the centre of which was a large crystal egg. It looked like a similar type of material to the Glass of the amulets, but it was corrupted, like the bodies of human women had been corrupted. Thick red veins ran through the stone, shifting like the shadows.

"The Ssscorpion crawlsss into our nessst," the first Birth-master hissed.

"What is that on her back?" the second boomed, his voice thundering through the chamber, shaking the crystal stalactites, causing scree to fall in its wake.

"She brought two more animals with her," the third whispered, and it sounded like it came from up close. Taberah almost felt the breath upon her ears.

"The Worm," the third Birth-master said, looking at Gouet. "And the Raven," he added, looking at Mudro.

"The Raven eats the Worm," the second bellowed.

The eyes of the first flashed, brightening up the chamber momentarily. "And the Ssscorpion ssstings them both."

"Enough word games," Gouet croaked. "They

don't have the same kind of power here as they do where we come from."

"But they do, Magus," the second thundered, "to those who come from where we come from."

Taberah did not engage with the Birth-masters. She had been warned about them before. She stayed out of sight, rummaging through her bags for her supplies. She took out a machine gun and its stand, and started to set it up.

"We found you," Mudro taunted, playing the game of time. "You survived by hiding, but we found your hiding place. What does that make you? Cowards?"

"We are Ssshadow," the first wheezed.

"And Rock," the second uttered.

"And Glass," the third sighed.

"You are demons," Mudro said, "and we're the exorcists."

Taberah fired the machine gun, which spat bullets out at a tremendous speed. There was so much kickback that even the legs of the stand quivered, and she found it difficult to turn and aim. The bullets sliced through anything they touched, smashing through crystals and punching holes in the granite wall. Yet when they came to the Birth-masters, they bounced off another crystalline structure that formed around them, as if they stood inside shields of Glass.

"Damn," she said, diving away as a crystal shard fired towards her from the staff of one of the Birth-masters. It struck the machine gun, which exploded into many shards of its own, discarding shell casings in all directions.

Taberah quickly crawled behind one of the larger

rocks, joining Mudro there.

"Well, that didn't work," she said.

Mudro looked like he desperately wanted to smoke. "I'm starting to think I might be lucky if I get to limp out of here."

"We need a little magic," Taberah suggested. "Machines are not enough here."

"How about a compromise?" Mudro replied, handing her a silver grenade, etched with many strange symbols. "That'll penetrate their shields. The gunpowder will do the rest."

"Good. How many have you got?"

"Just the one."

Taberah sighed. "Well, we better make the most of it then."

"You'll need to get close."

"How close?"

"Too close."

"Can you distract them?"

Mudro looked doubtful. "I can try."

Gouet must have had wonderful hearing for his age, because he started to make a great distraction of his own, rumbling out strange noises from the depths of his lungs, which seemed to grow as they left his mouth and echo throughout the chamber. A mighty wind blew with the sounds, crushing everything in its path, eroding rock and forcing the shields of the Birth-masters back a little.

Taberah charged out from her cover, running low, ducking and diving, and crawling her way from rock to rock, and crystal to crystal, until she was very close to the Birth-master that stood at the head of the triangle, and yet still further away than she would have liked. There was more natural cover further ahead, but she knew she could not get to it without being seen.

Then she smelled something familiar: the pungent aroma of the leaf. She turned and saw a stream of smoke wafting into the air from Mudro's position, like a smokey spotlight pinpointing where he was.

She peeped out at the Birth-masters and saw them aiming their staffs at the rock Mudro hid behind. As they concentrated their astral fire upon it, she dashed out, and dived behind the formation closer to the enemy, barely escaping notice. She sat with her back to the rock, watching as Mudro's cover was whittled down to nothing.

She bit her lip as she prepared to see her friend's noble sacrifice, but all that was left behind the stump of rock was his still-smoking pipe. She smiled. He was a pretty good illusionist after all.

She turned back to her mission, and glanced out. She was very close now, well within throwing distance. She pulled the pin and cast the grenade over, but it fell short of the target by just a few feet. If it had been anyone else, it would have been close enough to kill them, but it was just outside the shield of the Birth-master. Just outside was not good enough.

Taberah shook her head. "Damn it, I really wish we had Soasa now."

There were still seconds left on the clock before the grenade ignited. Taberah considered dashing towards it, but she knew she would not make it in time. Either the Birth-master would get her, or the blast would. She did not feel like following Soasa's exit from the world.

She took out her revolver and emptied the barrel into her hand, before replacing the metal casings with rubber pellets. They were practice ammunition, kept for making harmless warning shots, and she never really thought she would find a better use for them in battle.

She aimed her gun at the grenade and fired. The bullet struck the silver casing, denting it a little, and pushing it slightly closer to the Birth-master's shimmering crystal shield. He was so busy firing shards at the others that he did not notice the grenade creeping up beside him.

She fired again, and pushed it a little closer. The dents were becoming bigger, and she hoped her bullets would not pierce the shell. They might have been only rubber, but the force of the gunfire made them strike like steel.

The last few seconds were approaching. It all rested on this final shot. *Three.*

She clicked the trigger. *Two.* The bullet nudged the grenade just inside the shield, easily bypassing whatever protection the Birth-master had in place. *One.*

The explosion was a mix of machinery and magic, red fire joined with blue. They heard the Birth-master shriek, and it was neither a human nor a maran cry. The shadow on the wall convulsed and contorted, writhing about in a silhouette of agony. The crystalline shell fell apart like a smashed mirror, and all that was left upon the ground was a pile of sand and burnt robes.

The other two Birth-masters backed away.

It was then that the two Magi saw their opportunity, and came out from their cover. They advanced on the retreating Birth-masters, Gouet shouting words of power, and Mudro picking up the fallen staff. There were no buttons or triggers. It worked by will alone, and he willed it to end the lives of the demons.

The Birth-masters must have realised their doom was at hand, for they looked to one another, and seemed to agree something in their stare. One stepped forth to fight, while the other began to flee. Taberah charged after it.

The fighter reached his hands up to the air, until his fingers shook, and then the cavern roof shuddered, and the dangling stalactites trembled in place. Gouet weakened the demon's will with words, while Mudro weakened his body with crystal blades. He fired until there were as many embedded in his body as there were in the ceiling above.

Then the stalactites fell, and it was a shower of a thousand blades. Crystals sliced and smashed, and those that shattered sent out a thousand smaller blades, until there were few places that had not been stabbed with Glass. Gouet and Mudro tried to dodge, and tried to weaken, and tried to kill, but the hail hounded them, tearing through their clothes and slicing through their skin, until, by the time the Birth-master fell, Mudro had been weakened, and Gouet had been killed.

As the blades continued to fall, cutting off most routes into and out of the chamber, Taberah spotted the remaining Birth-master fleeing the scene.

"No!" she screamed, chasing the taunting shadow through the tunnel. She knew she could not let even one of the Birth-masters escape. She had to end their stranglehold. She had to end it once and for all.

Chapter Thirty-five

BROKEN GLASS

Taberah chased the Birth-master through the tunnel, ducking momentarily as it cast a crystal shard behind it from its staff. The shards were fewer now, and many of them broke apart mid-air. It seemed that the further he got from the others, the weaker he became.

Taberah replied with her pistol, never stopping to take aim. Bullets struck the cavern walls, missing the Birth-master. In a way, the further she got from the others, the weaker she became too, because she was running out of ammunition.

The tunnel dipped down, turned sharply several times, and then opened out into a gigantic mining chamber, one of the hundreds that burrowed through Landlock. She remembered them well from Project Glassfinder, when they secured enough Glass to make a hundred thousand amulets.

There were steps, bridges and passages all over the chamber, few with any safety rails. The Birth-master turned sharply left, slipping on some loose rock, and dropping his powerless staff in the process. He clambered up and raced across a short bridge made of wooden planks, which rocked beneath his weight.

Taberah followed him, trying to guess where he might run next. It was not an easy task, because it seemed like he had not been in this particular part of the cave network before. He was not powered by mind now, but instinct.

The Birth-master followed the closest wall, hugging the stone as he shimmied around on a narrow ledge. Taberah tried to grab him, but he reefed the arm of his robe from her grasp. She edged around after him, spotting him sliding down a ledge, the rock tearing his robes.

She dived after him, but now he was climbing up another rock face, heading towards one of the mining posts. She kept up the chase, but the gap was growing. He wanted to escape more than she wanted to catch him—and she wanted that a lot.

He knocked tools from the nearby tables as he passed. She leapt over them, grabbing a hammer from another table and hurling it at him. He yelped as it struck him in the back, but the pain only pushed him on, like a slave-driver.

He reached a set of stairs, taking two or three steps at a time. He turned sharply on a square platform, which had a deep drop on two sides. The stairs continued to the right, with more platforms at periodic intervals, littered with debris, tools, or containers.

There was enough of a gap now that he could take a moment to booby-trap the way. He grabbed a barrel from the next platform, filled with Glass crystals, and turned it on its side. As Taberah charged up the stairs after him, he kicked it down towards her.

The barrel thumped down the steps, gaining speed, and there was nowhere to go to avoid it but back down. Taberah raced back the way she had come, and the barrel broke apart on the final platform, half of it continuing over the ravine.

She turned back to the stairs and clambered over the shards, which sliced into her hands and knees. She gritted her teeth, focused her eyes on the fleeing Birth-master, and let every little pain and stumble nourish her anger. He was getting away, but she could not let him. She had to do this for her. She had to do this for Elizah. She had to do this for every woman, for every mother.

She darted up the steps again, watching him turn off to a wooden platform to the left, where the mining tracks for this chamber began. He struggled with the lever on the rusty mining cart there, saw her gaining on him, and abandoned that means of escape, returning to the ever-rising stairs.

He was close now, mere metres away, but if he matched her frenzied pace, he would still escape, and all of this would have been for nothing. Rommond might save the world from the bomb, but if she could not save it from this, none of it would matter. He tried to save the future of the world; she tried to save the future of humanity.

Her limbs ached, and her breath was painful. She breathed in slivers of Glass and iron, particles of sand and dust, and not enough air. Her mind hammered like a smithy, her heart like a piston. Part of her felt like she was the anvil, the passive slab against which the sword was honed—but another part felt like the sword.

He slipped on the steps, falling forward. Her eyes widened like a beast of prey, salivating at the stumble of the meal. He clambered up, and continued his flight, but the gap was narrower than ever. She could almost taste his fear, and she was glad that he was afraid.

The steps kept going, like a ladder to heaven—except they felt like they might die from exhaustion along the way. She chased the demon up, but thought that perhaps she should have been chasing it down instead.

Then he stopped suddenly and looked around frantically. She spotted the large gap in the platform ahead. There were only three ways to go now: turn back, jump across, or fall into the depths below. With her thundering up behind him, it was not much of a choice.

He readied himself for the leap, but she reached him before he could. She never slowed or stopped, but let the momentum strike him like a cannonball. She dived into him, grabbing him by the torso, and pulled him off the edge.

"It's over!" she spat into his ear as they fell.

She saw his demonic shadow try to crawl up the stone pillar, slipping constantly, with many gnarled hands reaching up, and clutching nothing.

The fall felt like forever. She loosened her grip on the Birth-master, and he tumbled away from her, but still he tumbled. No magic could stop that fall.

Then the Glass crystals at the bottom of the

ravine appeared like knives, and Taberah heard the crunch of the Birth-master's impact, before feeling the sharpened stalagmites rip through her own ribs. What little breath she had was knocked from her, and her torn lungs could not take another. The pounding of her heart increased for a moment, then suddenly abated, as if it too had taken its own great plunge. She lay on her back, bent and broken over the gigantic Glass crystal, the pain overcome by shock.

Her strength was failing quickly, but she had just enough left in her to turn her head slightly to the right, where she saw the broken body of the Birth-master, laid out on the torture rack of the earth. She gave the slightest of smiles. Then she felt a sudden tingling in her abdomen, and wondered if that was her injuries, or if it was what all human women were then feeling, the ability to conceive human children again.

Something caught her eye on the other side, and she turned slightly to it, and it took almost everything she had left to turn. Elizah stood there, older now, about the age she would have been if she had lived. She reached her hand out to her, and Taberah tried to touch it, but the darkness came then, and everything was swallowed up by the nothingness that ends it all.

Chapter Thirty-six

CRASH LANDING

Whistler knew he was running out of fuel, but he also knew that the bomb was slipping through everyone's fingers. He was not big or strong like most, and his grip was not great, but he did not have the luxury of letting go. He had to try, or fail. He kind of thought it likely he would fail, but when he saw Rommond and Jacob still keeping up their struggle, he knew he had to join the fight.

He flew beneath the Dreamdevil and tried to match its speed, but it was not an easy feat. Just as he got close, and fell beneath the shadow of the bomb, the larger plane jetted ahead suddenly, or he fell behind as the furnace burned low.

Even with the canopy closed, blocking out the howls of the wind, he could hear the straining wires. It was an awful sound that penetrated through the core of people, that worked its way into their bones. Yet, there was a noise more terrible that they tried to avoid—the sound of a world exploding.

At last, he managed to pull directly under the bomb, and push up enough to feel the wooden shell of his vessel touch the metal casing of the weapon. The agonising wail of the wires abated for a moment, replaced by the dreadful creaking of timber.

He held this position for what seemed like forever, rocking along the runway of the clouds. He knew he could not keep it up until the end of days, but he did not know how to let it down without simply dropping it.

The copter came around, and he saw Jacob and Rommond inside the tinted window. A mechanical arm extended, reaching its two metal fingers towards the bomb, holding it steady. He could see his comrades talking inside. He glanced towards the radio, but heard nothing. Maybe they had a plan—but he did not know what they wanted to do.

He felt the Dreamdevil dip slightly, pushing him down, pushing all of them down. He wondered if that was the plan, to try to land together, every vessel holding hands tightly.

A thick cloud stood like a wall up ahead, and they flew straight towards it, unable to turn sharply, or rise quickly, or fall rapidly. The white hue smothered them all, forcing them to rely on instinct, on sound and feel. He could still hear the creaking wood, and could still feel the weight of the world above him.

Yet the cloud did not cushion them. It shook the aircraft, steadily at first, then more violently as they continued to disappear into it. They had no idea where they were going, and sound and feel was starting to be drowned out by the shaking of their vessels.

Then Whistler heard a sudden, sharp snap of wire, like iron lightning. He saw a flicker of black across his field of view, and heard the sound of a cable tangling with metal blades, like iron thunder. There was an explosion ahead, which rattled his monoplane, and sent out a black cloud to penetrate the pallid fog.

"Jacob," he called into the radio, but there was no response.

A blade from the copter's main propeller flung against the canopy of his plane, scratching the glass before blowing away with a clatter of wind. There were many other sounds, of struggling engines and failing parts, but he tried not to listen too closely to them.

They'll be all right, he tried to reassure himself. *We'll be all right.*

The bomb weighed more heavily on him than before. There was just a single wire securing it to the Dreamdevil, and he heard its wind-piercing whine, like the taunts of a hundred thousand dead.

Then it snapped.

"Oh, God," he blurted, feeling the weight of the bomb pushing the plane down, like the mighty finger of a god trying to crush him. Though the weapon rested on the straining wooden frame of his aeroplane, it kind of felt like it rested directly on him, like it was on his shoulders, on his back.

He tried to pull up, but nothing could resist the awful push of the bomb, or the awful pull of gravity. In the sky he felt at home, powerful, but now he felt entirely powerless, hunted back to the earth by the real powers of the air.

He glanced at the fuel meter, where the needle flickered in the red zone. He wished he had not seen it, but kept looking back and forth between the needle and the still great distance between him and land.

He did not want to think it, but the thoughts exploded in his mind: *I'm not going to make it.*

He grabbed the radio, and clicked the button. He heard the phantom voice of static.

"I'm almost out of fuel," he said, his voice shaking. The radio shook in his hand too.

There was no reply.

He felt a sudden well of tears, and gulped down the lump in his throat. The sky did not scare him. Even the fall did not frighten him. The silence did.

He waited for a moment, even though there was really no time for waiting.

"Guys?" he asked the radio. He hoped he was asking his friends, but it felt like he was just talking to metal. Even the static did not seem to pay him any heed.

He had always felt alone, no matter how many people there were around him. Yet at that moment, with the world fast approaching, and not a waking soul in sight or sound, he never felt so lonely. He gripped the control stick—not for steering, but for support. He would have rather gripped someone's hand. Maybe it might have been his mother's. Maybe Jacob's instead. It almost did not matter. And yet—everything in those fleeting moments mattered more than most.

The flat fields seemed to rise like mountains, and the sky fell suddenly away, the clouds fleeing from him, and from that awful world-swallowing cloud that would soon follow. He descended faster, the bomb pushing him towards his doom. That he would be the first it claimed was perhaps inconsequential in the end, but it was significant to him.

Whistler closed his eyes, and tried not to feel the sinking or the rumble, or the pressure, or even his heaving heart. He wanted to think of something good. He wanted his final thought to be a happy one. He searched his mind, but was constantly dragged back to the sinking and the rumbling.

Then he felt a sudden lift in the pressure, and he thought that he had somehow bypassed the explosion, that he was now ascending to heaven. He opened his eyes and looked up, and he saw the struggling copter, bleeding black smoke, its mechanical arm clutching the tail of the bomb.

His plane descended much more slowly now, the bomb pulling on the copter instead of pushing on his hull. Yet it still fell, and he did not have enough fuel left to fight against the fall. The ground did not rise as swiftly, but it still rose towards him.

He was startled by something that struck the canopy, and was surprised to see Jacob there, clutching the glass. The smuggler bashed against the window, holding up a bag of coal in his other hand.

Whistler unlatched the canopy, and pushed it up. Jacob hopped inside. It was a tight fit, not designed for two pilots like the larger plane used by Trokus. But it beat hanging on outside.

"Phew!" Jacob said. "Remind me never to do this again."

Whistler smiled at Jacob. He did not really know what to say.

"Sorry," Jacob said, pushing the boy to one side.

He tore open the bag of coal and fired it, bag and all, into the dying furnace, which spluttered to life immediately.

Whistler saw the needle of the fuel meter rise a little. Not a lot, but he thought it might just be enough. He pulled up, and the plane obeyed.

"It's working!" he cried to Jacob.

Jacob glanced up through the canopy, where he could see Rommond in the copter, struggling to keep his grip on the bomb. The general looked at him, and did not look confident that they would make it in the end.

"Well," Jacob said, holding out his hand to Whistler. "If this is how it all ends, it's good to end it with a friend."

Whistler took his hand and smiled. From the corner of his eye, he saw the ground reach up to grab them. He held his breath, and felt the welling up of every buried fear. The plane did not so much as land as crash, breaking apart as it bounced off the ground.

Chapter Thirty-seven

WAKE-UP CALL

Jacob and Whistler were thrown from the wreckage of the monoplane. They tumbled across the desert, covered by the tossing sands and splintering wood. Jacob landed on his back, facing the angry gaze of the sun.

He groaned, and heard Whistler moan beside him. He was so preoccupied with his own aching body that for a moment he forgot about the bomb. Then the thought exploded in his mind and he sat up suddenly, forcing his muscles to spasm.

The stabbing sunshine and the sandy haze made it difficult to see, but soon he found a broken wing, and then the rest of the plane, and further up the copter, with some propellers still spinning, and further still: the bomb, half-submerged in sand.

He shook his head in disbelief. *We did it.*

Whistler sat up, sobbing as he clutched his skint and bruised arm.

"You okay?" Jacob asked him.

"Yeah," the boy said, shaking sand from his hair. "You?"

Jacob nodded emphatically. "You know what … I am. We all are. It … it didn't go off." He let out the greatest sigh he had ever made in his life, and he felt like he exhaled sand as well as air. Indeed, he felt like he let out a lot of his troubles. They did not seem so great in comparison to that bulbous weapon.

"We did it," Whistler said. His smile was like a fairer kind of sunshine.

A hatch on the copter opened suddenly, and out stumbled Rommond, beating away the smoke and sand with his cap. He stopped, scanned the area, spotted the bomb, and then saw them.

"Not bad for a day's work, eh?" Jacob shouted over to him.

"Not bad at all," the general replied, placing his cap back on and straightening it up.

He stopped beside them and stood with his hands behind his back, surveying the site.

"I guess we *can* make a difference," Whistler said.

"Was that ever in doubt?" Rommond asked.

"I think everything was in doubt," Jacob replied.

"We did a remarkable deed here. One that will go down in history. Or, if I had my way, one that we could erase from history. That weapon needs to be dismantled. This was a wake-up call for me. I hope it was for everyone else. We cannot allow this kind of weapon to be used in this war, or any other. We'll have to kill each other a different way."

Jacob got up and helped Whistler to his feet. The trio approached the bomb slowly, afraid that, after everything, somehow even a whisper might set it off.

"Our greatest success," Jacob said.

"My greatest failure," the general replied. "I should have never dreamed of this."

"Someone else would have, surely."

"Would have, might have, maybe ... who knows? All I know is that I gave the order. I approved the project. I funded the science. I betrayed us all with those decisions, so I guess they weren't really wrong when they drew me as a demon. I almost sent us all to Hell."

"But you didn't," Jacob said. "And you helped stop this thing."

Rommond turned to Whistler. "I think our little lord of the sky had a lot to do with that."

Whistler blushed and simpered.

Then they heard a sudden cry from far afield, and Rommond immediately unearthed his pistol. The haze of sand was still thick, and though it offered good cover from watchful eyes, it offered none from darting bullets.

A man came through the haze, half-prancing and half-floundering, his arms waving madly about, and his long coat waving with them. It was Porridge.

"Oh!" he cried, running over to the broken copter. "My baby!" He collapsed dramatically to his knees, as if it really was his fallen child.

"You can make another one," Rommond said, strolling over to him and placing a hand upon his shoulder. Porridge gripped the general's hand with his, as if Rommond had been the father.

"Oh, it's dreadful! But at least it's over, darling. We're all lucky lemons indeed!" Porridge pulled out of Rommond's arm until he was standing again, and then continued to hang out of the general's uniform, stumbling in his heels as Rommond brought him away from the fire and smoke of the copter. Jacob went to help, and Porridge grabbed a hold of the smuggler's arm. "Oh, my ripened raspberries, you're a muscly one!"

Jacob raised an eyebrow, and Whistler grinned at him.

All four of them sat together away from the wreckage, wondering what they were going to do next. They were not entirely sure where they were, but they knew they had landed in Regime territory. None of the flying vessels were in good enough condition to fly again, and the sand was not a good choice for a runway.

"We might have to walk it," Jacob said.

"In these!" Porridge protested, emptying sand from one of his shoes.

"We can't leave the bomb unattended," Rommond replied.

Jacob shielded his eyes from the sun. It was getting low now, which was probably worse, because then the bitter cold of night would follow. "We can't survive long out here either."

"Maybe we won't have to," Whistler said, pointing to the horizon.

There, attracted by the many plumes of smoke, were the silhouettes of half a dozen vehicles, racing swiftly towards them, bearing the unmistakable emblem of the Regime.

Chapter Thirty-eight

UNDOING PROGRESS

"Get ready for a fight," Rommond said, taking his pistol out again.

The trucks and landships approached, halting within firing range. They paused there for a moment, their barrels aimed, facing off against the general's handgun. It seemed like at any moment either of them would shoot.

Then the door of one of the trucks opened, and out stepped Trokus.

"You!" Rommond barked. "Seems you got here a lot more comfortably than we did."

The commander strolled over, with two guards at his sides. Jacob wondered why he bothered with them. The general would take out all three of them before the first turret fired.

"The scientists," Rommond said. "Where are they?"

"We have them in safe-keeping."

"There's a safer place. It's about six feet below."

"The bunker we all go to eventually, eh?"

"Amusing," Rommond said. "Perhaps you'll forgive my lack of humour at the moment. You see, I'm rather under the impression that you betrayed us.

And that makes my finger itchy."

"I had to," Trokus explained. "I was under orders."

"My finger's under orders. At the moment, those are: *let him speak*. But orders change."

"They had my wife and daughter."

"This bomb had the world."

"Family's everything to me," Trokus said, and his lip trembled. "I tried to tell you that. I lost my boy up there. I couldn't lose the others. I had to do what the Iron Emperor wanted. He wanted the scientists. He knew you'd stop the bomb."

"So, what is this, your apology?"

"In a way, yes. I just wanted you to know that I didn't do it. I didn't hand them over. I sent decoys instead. I hope he doesn't notice, because I dread to think of what he'll do. I got my wife and child back, but I know that he can take them again. His reach … it's the distance of the world."

Rommond lowered his gun. "Where are the real scientists?"

Trokus gestured towards one of the trucks, and before he was finished gesturing, Rommond opened fire on it, until there were no more bullets in his gun.

"Are you mad?" Trokus shouted. "I'm trying to do the decent thing here! I'm giving you them! I only took them to get my family back."

Rommond breathed heavy. Jacob could tell that if he had another weapon, he would have unloaded that one too. He saw him eyeing the guns of the guards. It must have taken a lot of restraint not to make a move.

"Why are you helping us?" Jacob asked.

"Because up there you showed me who you really

are. When my son's plane went down, your Whistler went down to save him, and you went down to save them both. That's the kind of thing families do, no matter what the cost. I guess you're a kind of family after all."

"Touching," Rommond said, "but how do we know this is not another ruse? How do we know the Iron Emperor isn't controlling your tongue once again?"

"Maybe a gesture will help." Trokus turned and nodded to one of the men standing by his truck. He opened the door, and out stepped Brooklyn.

"We found him wandering in Regime territory."

The pistol fell from Rommond's grip, and he almost fell with it. It was Porridge's turn to hold him up, and he could barely do that for himself. Brooklyn started to run towards the general, and Rommond followed suit, until they embraced each other in the middle.

Yet, Rommond being Rommond, he spared little time for that embrace, and none for pleasantries. He pointed to the bomb. "Can you dismantle it?"

"I am not sure," Brooklyn said. "These spirits are different kind. I need time to learn dialect."

"Okay, but make it quick. The sooner this thing is destroyed, the better."

"It is odd for me to be unmaking instead of making."

"Consider it making parts."

Brooklyn walked towards the bomb and sat down beside it, beginning his long process of meditation. Rommond did not like it, because it took too long.

Every second could have been the finger on the button, but the seconds passed, and they were still there.

Rommond returned to Trokus. "You surprised me yet."

"So did you. I never thought you'd propose a truce."

"So, is this a truce?"

"Not between you and the Iron Empire. But between us, yes. We don't answer to the Iron Emperor any more."

"A wise decision."

"I'm not sure it's wise, but … here we are." He held his hand out to the general.

Rommond eyed him up and down, then took Trokus' hand and pulled him close. "I hope I don't regret this."

"I hope I don't regret it either."

Rommond paused mid-shake. "The scientists."

Trokus nodded. "They're yours."

"No," the general said. "They belong to Death."

When Brooklyn finished his meditation, he had learned the dialect of the spirits of the bomb.

"I need uniform," he told the Regime soldiers. "Heavy uniform." He circulated several designs, which were passed to outfitters, who were more ac-customed to protecting people from bullets, not radiation. Yet they had faced these troubles before in smaller form, when the trenches were bombarded with nerve gas and other toxins, and it did not take long before a combined human and maran team developed protective clothing to encase the tribesman.

It took several days for Brooklyn to understand the bomb, and several more to take it apart. It was a nerve-racking process, more like a surgical operation than anything else. There were several helpers, bringing tools in, and taking away delicate parts, and it was clear from the constant expression of apprehension on their faces that none of them wanted to be there.

When the dismantling was over, there were thousands of tiny little pieces, arranged carefully in boxes for hazardous and non-hazardous material, which were hauled out in trucks, carts, wheelbarrows, and in jittering hands. A panic almost started when one box was inadvertently dropped. The battle in the sky was over, but everyone still felt hounded by the bomb.

"We need to bury the pieces," Rommond said. "We can't afford anyone assembling this jigsaw again."

"Surely it'll be hard to find all the pieces," Jacob said.

"Perhaps, but we don't want them even finding half of them. If you see enough of the picture, the puzzle becomes a lot easier to solve."

"Where do we bury them?" Brooklyn asked.

"Everywhere," the general said. "Bring some to your people to distribute in the land. I'll get a lot of it out to sea, and hopefully the fishes will eat it up in these nice bite-sized chunks. We'll have to dig deep in the dunes to hide the rest. Only a select few can know where we're hiding it. I don't ever want to see or hear about this weapon ever again."

A giant bonfire was arranged in the desert, which Doctor Elbern and Doctor Ekar were forced to contribute to. Both humans and marans heaved stacks of papers by the wheelbarrow, parking them beside the burgeoning flames.

"You can't," Elbern said. "I spent my entire life on this."

"Funny how easily it all burns," Rommond said. "Just like the many people you would have condemned to the flames."

"This was *your* idea."

"Which I ordered you to abandon."

The doctor looked Rommond up and down. "You didn't have the courage."

"I didn't have the madness."

"We could have ended this war," Elbern said. "In one big puff of smoke."

Rommond frowned. "But this is just a dream … remember?"

"We could have ended this dream." He nudged his brother, but Ekar said nothing.

"The end is coming … for some."

"You need me," Elbern told him. There was a time when Rommond believed it, when he thought that maybe there really was no other option to defeat the demons.

"Oh, really?" the general replied.

"What if the demons find a way to make it again?"

"But Doctor … *I'm* the demon, don't you recall?"

Elbern shook his head violently, his dishevelled

hair flaying from side to side. "I'm the only person left who knows how to make this." His brother did not protest, but Rommond knew that he had as much knowledge of the bomb as Elbern did.

"Good," Rommond replied, unloading a single bullet between the doctor's eyes. Ekar watched his brother stumbled forward, and then he tried to run, but the bullet ran faster. As the bodies fell to the ground, their glasses cracking in the fall, Rommond thought that maybe now they could all sleep a little sounder.

Chapter Thirty-nine

HATE

Everyone returned to the safety of Blackout, though it was strange that "everyone" included so many people they had at one time called demons. Rommond was keen to keep that under wraps. He knew that distrust was still high. It was high in him as well.

Leadman made his last delivery to the city, having had to trek back and forth to Commspire Oasis to secure as much of its communications equipment as possible. Rommond authorised Tardo to set up a new listening post in the old clock tower, and Tardo gleefully complied. He hurried back and forward to collect new toys from the overflowing toybox Leadman kept topping up.

After the final shipment, when Tardo could clearly visualise the new array, his excitement became so much that he got clumsy. He stepped back to view the full collection, only to stumble into Gregan.

"Watch where you're going," Gregan barked.

"Oh! I'm sorry! I didn't see you th—"

"Well, you've got eyes, don't you? Or do demons have something else?"

"Eh—"

"You think you can just march around like you own the place."

"No, I—"

"You think you don't need to mind where you look, 'cause sure it's only humans in the way, right?"

Tardo shook his head.

"What, you not going to answer me now?"

"I'm sorry, I really don't—"

"We oughta teach you a lesson!"

"But I'm on your side!" Tardo exclaimed.

"You ain't on our side," Gregan spat. "This side's for our kind. You ain't our kind. You ain't even close."

"But I'm fighting for you ... *with* you."

"Stop it!" Whistler cried, forcing himself between the two men. He looked up at Gregan, who towered over him, and he almost regretted doing anything at all.

"Get out of the way, boy."

"No!"

"This isn't your fight, boy. Get out of the way."

"If you're going to pick a fight with a demon, then pick one with me!"

Gregan's face contorted. "So *you're* the half-blood." He prodded Whistler in the shoulder with a stabbing finger. "I don't know what sickens me more. The scum, or the spawn of the scum. Everything about you, boy, is wrong."

Whistler tried to hold back his tears, to stop the tremble of his mouth. He wanted to be brave for Tardo, who was being brave for the Resistance, fighting against his own people. Whistler never thought he would have to do the same.

"You come here," Gregan bellowed at Tardo. Whistler closed his eyes as the spit covered his face. "You kill our men. You rape our women. And you mix your own with ours and try and pass 'em off as human?"

By now Whistler was shaking, clenching his fists to try and stop the shudders.

Leadman walked by, casting the word "Lieutenant" over his shoulder, like a hook to catch a fish. Gregan grumbled and began to back away, but as he did so he pointed the blade of his finger at Gregan and Whistler, and equally the blade of his tongue.

"You just wait," he hissed, and never was waiting more of a threat. They had been waiting for the bomb, but as Whistler looked up to Gregan's pale face, he felt that maybe there was something just as destructive in the hearts of men.

The final delivery did not come from Commspire Oasis, but from Fort Landlock.

"Where's Tabs?" Rommond asked.

Leadman took off his cap and bowed his head.

Rommond shook his own. "You were supposed to look after her."

"That wasn't my mission," Leadman replied. "She made it clear that the last leg of the journey was her own. I'm surprised any of them got out of that cavern." He turned to Mudro.

"She finished what she started," he said. "It wasn't for nothing."

"Her body?" Rommond asked.

"It's … she's in the Silver Ghost."

Rommond looked at the silver warwagon, with its lanterns still burning brightly. She had spent so much time operating out of it that it was essentially her portable home. He remembered unveiling it. It was a gift for her. Now it was her mausoleum.

The general sighed. "Will there be any of us left?" He knew they could not answer. Maybe he was just asking himself. Maybe he was asking the gods. Either way, no one replied.

Rommond looked at them with grim determination. "Don't tell the boy."

"He has a right to know," Mudro said.

"It doesn't matter if he has the right. He's a sensitive one. He has no family left."

"What about the smuggler?"

"He's not family."

"No, I mean, what if he tells the boy?"

"Does Jacob know?"

"Not yet."

"Then don't tell him either."

Life was getting back to normal in Blackout, but many were still restless, as if there was still a Dreamdevil up above, still a bomb left to drop. In the Olive Inn, Whistler found it difficult to sleep. He considered knocking in at Jacob's room to see if he was up, but felt it was unfair to wake him.

He sat on the wooden chair by the window, gazing out at the night sky, musing about its vastness, wondering if there were other worlds out there, and other peoples, and thinking that maybe on one of them there was another boy looking out and wondering the same.

For a moment, he thought he heard his mother's voice. He turned around, but there was no one there. He thought he must have been imaging it. It would not have been the first time. She had been gone a while now. That was not the first time either.

He turned back to the sights of nature. There were parts of Blackout where the smog was not so thick, and the sounds were not so industrial. Nature had a way of creeping into everything, growing through the cracks in bricks, adapting to the iron.

He was so enraptured by the sound of the crickets and the owls that he did not hear the creaking of the floorboard behind him. He was so enamoured by the sight of the sky that he did not see the reflection of a figure in the window. His bare arms rested on the sill, his head bobbed to one side, exposing his neck, which his reddish-brown curls tried to hide. Then he felt a strong arm around his neck, and a strong hand around his mouth, and he tried to scream as he was dragged off into the darkness, where the only witnesses were the crickets and the owls.

Chapter Fourty

INSTINCT

Jacob's sleep was as restless as ever, and he could not think why. With the greatest threat to Altadas disarmed, he should have finally gotten a much-deserved good night's sleep. He tossed and turned, pushing the bedsheets off, and pulling them back over him when it got cold again. When he eventually dozed off, he awoke from a swiftly forgotten nightmare. He sat up, sweating, watching the shifting darkness in the room. He thought he heard a sound, like a muffled cry, but presumed he was imagining things. The moments after a nightmare always seemed ripe for the imagination.

Jacob lay back down, but something told him he had to investigate the noise. He put on a night coat and slippers, and peeked his head out into the corridor. There was no one there. The moon cast a faint glow through an open window at the end, and the wind gently caressed the curtains.

You're going mad, Jacob thought. *Guess Cala's had an effect on you after all.*

He decided to go back to bed, but as he was closing his door he heard a thump. He darted out into the corridor and halted there, realising he probably should have brought a weapon. He could not explain why. Blackout was under Resistance control now, and the Baroness had worked hard on improving security. Hell, Rommond slept in that same inn. That was the definition of safe. Yet something did not feel right. Jacob's mind told him he was overreacting, but his heart told him he was not doing enough.

He listened again for the noise. It was lower this time, a weaker thump, as if it came from further away. Yet it sounded close enough that Jacob was certain that it came from somewhere in the building. He raced back into his room, grabbed the gun from his bedside locker, and rushed back into the corridor to investigate. As he did, he realised how things had changed. Only a year before, he would have dismissed this as someone else's problem.

He walked slowly through the corridor, straining his hearing. It was silent now. He headed towards the stairs to the next level, in case the sound was coming from downstairs. Everything seemed quiet there. He waited for a moment, keeping one hand on the bannister, the other on the trigger.

Another thump, fainter than before. It seemed to be coming from the direction of Whistler's room, back down the hall from where he had come. Part of him thought that there was likely a logical explanation, that the boy could not sleep either. Another part, the part that made him get his gun, told him it was something more.

He reached the door of Whistler's room and placed his ear against the wood. He worried if this was an invasion of privacy. Hell, he would not have wanted anyone listening in on him for half the nights he stayed in the Olive Inn, with a telltale coat hanger on the doorknob. The landlord should have charged him double rent.

Jacob gently rapped his knuckles on the door. "Everything okay in there?"

There was another thump, very weak now. It seemed the closer Jacob got, the fainter it became.

He tried the handle of the door, but it was locked. Whistler did not usually lock his door. He was always eager for company.

"Whistler?" Jacob said, knocking on the door again. "You okay, kid?"

There was no sound now.

Hell, Jacob thought. Something told him he had to break in, and he had to do it now.

He pushed against the door with his shoulder. It would not budge. He shoved again, harder, and the hinges strained. He got a bit of a run up to it next, denting the wood, but it still held strong.

Then he fired two rounds at the lock, blasting it apart. He shoved the door open, and dropped the gun to the floor.

In the centre of the room, near a fallen chair, Whistler hung from the lamp shade of the oil lamp attached to the ceiling, a thick rope around his neck, his head bobbed to the side, his eyes closed, his mouth open, his arms limp, and his legs dangling.

Chapter Forty-one

WAKE

Jacob darted forward, grabbing the boy's legs and pushing him upward, trying to release the tugging on his neck. There was no reaction from the child, not a twitch, nor a sound of choking, nor a hint of wheezing.

"Help!" the smuggler shouted. He had to get the boy down, but also had to hold him up. If he let go now, that could be the end of it. He tried to smother the thought that none of it mattered, that he was already too late.

"Help!" he repeated, more forcefully and more desperately. Everything seemed to be passing slowly. Even his own cries seemed drawn out.

He struggled to hold up the child and free him from his noose, and could not help but think of the boy's own struggle, of all the thumps he made as the rope grew tighter, and the air grew less.

Why did you delay? Jacob berated himself.

He stretched his foot towards the chair lying on its side, which Whistler must have leapt from. It was just an inch out of reach. Jacob tried to stretch a little further, painfully aware that he had to release the boy a little to do it. He finally reached it, and tugged it

239

closer with his toes.

"Help!" he cried again, but no one was helping. No one was coming. This moment of desperation was for him alone. He had to hold Whistler up. He had to get Whistler down. He had to cope with the constant realisation that all those thumping sounds were for him to listen to, and him to act on.

Why did you delay?

He wrestled the fallen chair with his foot, trying to nudge it up. Whistler's body swayed in his arms, and the rope swayed, and the lampshade swayed. He tried again to pull the chair up, and managed to get it upright. He used his knees to move it into place beneath Whistler's dangling feet. Even then it was not enough. The boy was too short to stand on the chair and reach the noose. He must have stood on the back of the seat instead.

Jacob shuffled around, still clutching Whistler's legs, and ushered him up higher, taking a step of his own onto the chair. He tried to rest the boy's feet on the back, but they slipped off. There was no strength in him. Jacob was frightfully aware that if he lost his grip on the boy, he would slip again, and the force of the fall could snap his neck.

He held him tight in one arm, resting the boy's weight against his chest and shoulder, while he reached up with the other hand to try to loosen the knot. He could not see where he was stretching. Whistler's body slumped down on him, blocking his view. It was a scramble of seconds, each finger reaching for the rope, fumbling for the knot, feeling the warmth of the boy's body, and fearing it was going cold.

Finally, he seized the knot and pulled. It resisted. Instead of pulling it loose, he thought he might have just pulled it a little tighter. He was glad then that the boy was thin, that he could still fit his thumb between the rope and Whistler's neck. He was glad that the boy was light, that he could still haul him up in one hand while he desperately tried to free him with the other.

The knot came loose, and he tumbled backwards off the chair, the boy falling with him. His back slammed against the floor, knocking the breath from him, and though pain raced through his body, his sole focus was Whistler, and the breath he was not taking.

He rolled over, placing Whistler on his back. The boy did not budge. Not a twitch of an eyelid. Not the spasm of a muscle. His reddish-brown hair was wet from sweat, and there was what appeared to be a fresh cut across his temple, like the mark of a fingernail. Jacob could only imagine it was from the desperate last-minute thrashing he made as his instinct for survival kicked in.

Jacob did not feel for a pulse. He feared he might not find one. He tried to remember what to do in situations like this. He had not received the basic medical training that soldiers do. He recalled snippets of what he saw others do with those who collapsed or almost drowned. He hoped the snippets were enough.

He pressed his hands on the boy's chest, trying to get his lungs pumping. He heard sounds from downstairs, and rushing footsteps growing closer. Rommond appeared in the hallway, pistol in hand.

"God," he blurted.

"Get the nurse!" Jacob cried.

Rommond rushed back outside. The sound of his boots thundering down the stairs echoed through the corridor.

Jacob pumped Whistler's chest again, and placed his ear close to the boy's mouth, listening for a breath. Nothing came. He pinched the boy's nose and breathed into his mouth. Then he pressed on Whistler's chest once more.

"Stay with me, kid," he pleaded, running his hand through his own sweat-laden hair in exasperation.

He thought he felt a slight shudder in the boy's body, but he was not sure if that was just a reflex from everything Jacob was doing to try to get him breathing again. He knelt beside him, cradling his neck, unsure of what else he could do.

Stay with me.

He heard a clamour of doors slamming, feet stomping, and raised voices downstairs. Before he knew it, he looked up to see Lorelai crouching down beside them, emptying out her bag of medical supplies on the floor.

"Get his shirt off," she ordered. Her voice seemed a little distant, even though she was right there beside him. It took a moment for her words to register.

He tore Whistler's patched shirt open. The buttons flew off in all directions, spinning and sliding across the floor. One rolled towards the window, spun on its side for what seemed like a lifetime, then fell flat with a thud.

The boy looked so frail beneath his clothes, even though he was so much worse when Jacob first met him, all those months ago in the Hold. The colour was fading from him, highlighting the thick red marks around his neck.

Lorelai prepped an innovative electrical device known as a heart-hopper. It was a collection of exposed wires, nestled into a box with a large battery. One of the wires had a rubber pad on the end. She adjusted many knobs and dials. It was almost like a radio. Jacob could not help but think that maybe she was listening for the frequency of his heart.

Rommond stood in the threshold of the door, stopping a throng of people behind him from entering. He seemed to be scanning the room with his eyes, and they finally settled on the discarded rope.

"Who told him?" he barked to those behind him. "Who?"

There was a flurry of defensive remarks, and the tumult of voices faded into one another, until it all sounded like background noise to Jacob, until it all sounded like radio static.

Jacob's focus was stolen by the sudden jerk of Whistler's body as Lorelai pressed the wire and rubber pad against his chest. The boy convulsed, then fell flat, his head falling back into Jacob's hand.

Jacob bit his lip to stop it from trembling.

Stay with me.

The nurse repeated the procedure, and the result was the same. For a fraction of a second, it almost seemed like the boy came to life again. His limbs flayed, and his head rose. Then, just as quickly, he fell still again.

She tried once more, and the chatter of those at the door grew silent.

Lorelai gave an audible sigh. Her shoulders drooped, and the electrical device slid from her hand. She looked at Jacob, and he looked at her. He held his breath, and she shook her head.

Chapter Fourty-two

WHY?

Whistler suddenly gasped for breath. His body spasmed, and his eyes blinked open. He took several sharp lungfuls of air, coughing and sputtering. He squinted his eyes as the light attacked them, and he looked about at everyone present with confusion etched as clearly as the rope marks.

Jacob could not hold back his smile, or the tear that rolled down his cheek and leapt to the floor. He wanted to say everything, but found he could say nothing. The unshed tears clogged his throat. As the boy regained his breath, Jacob barely breathed at all.

Rommond ushered the other people outside, while Lorelai started to tidy up her tools.

"He needs rest," she said as she worked.

Whistler groaned as Jacob picked him up and placed him gently on the bed. The smuggler fluffed the pillows and propped up the boy's head. He had never been so gentle in his life.

"Why?" Jacob asked, lightly touching the back of his index and middle fingers to the red blotches on the boy's neck.

Whistler grimaced, closing his eyes tight. It took a moment for the boy to focus on him.

"You have so much to live for," Jacob said.

Whistler's words were a struggle. "I didn't ..."

"It's okay," Jacob said. "It doesn't matter why."

"I ... didn't ... do it," the boy gasped.

"I don't understand."

"I didn't," the boy began, swallowing hard, "want to die."

Jacob shook his head. *Then why?* he thought.

"It was him," Whistler said.

Jacob took the half-filled glass of water from the bedside locker and handed it to the boy. Whistler took it with a quivering hand and gulped down a mouthful.

"It was who?" Jacob asked. He brushed an auburn curl from Whistler's eye.

"One of ... Leadman's guys."

"Gregan?"

"Yeah."

"He ... he tied you up there?"

Whistler nodded. The fear was still in his eyes.

Jacob looked towards the door. Lorelai was still there, clutching her medical supplies to her chest, watching them with worried eyes.

"I'll let the general know," she said, then left the room.

Jacob turned back to Whistler. The boy grabbed his hand and held it as tight as his strength would allow.

"You're safe now," Jacob reassured him. It seemed like an empty statement, but he felt he had to say something. Whistler should have been safe before. This was Resistance territory. These were Resistance men. They should have been able to depend on them.

The fear never left Whistler's eyes.

"Why do people hate?" the boy asked. "I don't understand it."

"It doesn't make any more sense when you get older," Jacob said.

"They hate me because I'm a demon."

"But you're not, not even half. We have to stop using that word. You're part-human and part-maran. And there's nothing wrong with that. But him. He's all demon. It was the demon in him that made him do this."

"The demons don't scare me," Whistler sobbed. "The humans do."

"I know. It's all wrong. Some of the people we're fighting against are better than we are, and some of the people fighting on our side are the worst I've seen. There's no black and white in war, even though people try to make us think there is. It brings out the best in some, and the worst in others. I hate that we can't depend on people."

"I don't want to hate him."

"I do," Jacob said.

"Don't," Whistler pleaded, squeezing his hand tighter. "I don't want hate to come from me, or because of me. It doesn't make any of it better. It just makes everything worse."

Jacob sighed. "Yeah. I guess you're right."

Rommond made no delay in storming the building where Leadman and his men resided. He made sure it was surrounded before breaking down the door.

"Where is he?" he growled, crunching splinters beneath his boots.

The people inside stirred from their sleep, coming down the stairs with their pistols ready. They presumed the city was under attack.

"What's all this ruckus?" Leadman asked, covering up a yawn.

"Where's Gregan?" Rommond barked.

"He should be in his quarters. Why?"

Rommond thundered up the stairs, pushing past Leadman. He forced open the door to Gregan's room, but it was empty.

Leadman strolled up beside him. "What's all this about, Rommond?"

"He tried to kill Brogan."

"Taberah's kid?"

"Yes."

"Blimey. Are you sure?"

"I trust the boy's word."

"Maybe you shouldn't," Leadman said. "Unless you've forgotten how much of a liar you were when you were a boy."

"Brogan's not like you and I. It's not his nature to lie."

"Fair enough. I'll see that Gregan is disciplined."

"No," Rommond said, shaking his head violently, and stabbing his chest with his index finger. "*I'll* see that he's disciplined."

"That's not your call, Rommond. He's one of my men."

"Yet another reason why we shouldn't trust you."

"You'd want to watch that tongue of yours. You've

flown mighty high these last few years, but your wings can still be clipped."

Rommond glared at him. "There was a saying in the trenches—"

"You and your sayings," Leadman interjected, rolling his eyes.

"—He who is loyal to the conman and the criminal shares in their crimes."

"If you're trying to suggest that I was somehow complicit in Gregan's actions, if indeed they were even his actions, you are very much mistaken. I've risked a lot coming here to help you win this war. I can't help but feel that maybe you're not doing your part to uphold the bargain."

"I've always done my part."

"I have reserves coming in from Copperfort in a few days. Why should I station them here?"

"Don't make this about you and I," Rommond barked.

"I didn't. You did."

The general's glare was penetrating. "If you want a little war between us, then you'll have your little war. And maybe Gregan can stand in the no man's land between us. That way he'll die to both our bullets."

HOMECOMING

B rooklyn arrived back in Blackout from his final work disarming the bomb that same night, and was surprised at the commotion. He did not find Rommond in the Olive Inn, where he expected, but in the war room below ground, brooding over a worn map of Altadas.

"Edward."

Rommond turned to him, and smiled. "You're back."

"You never asked if all of me came back."

The general bit his lip. "I was afraid to."

Brooklyn smiled. "You did not need to be afraid." He sat down beside the general and placed his hand on his. "Always thinking of the next battle, hmm?"

"War is not for the weary," Rommond said. "We rest in death."

There was a knock on the door, and Jacob came inside.

"Is he okay?" Rommond asked.

"Yeah. He's sleeping now. Lorelai is watching him."

"I put a guard on his room, and on the inn," the general said.

"I saw."

"What happened?" Brooklyn asked.

"One of Leadman's men," Rommond replied, shaking his head. "I can't believe he'd do that to a kid."

"Little Brogan? He is hurt?"

"Not as hurt as Gregan will be."

"That's why I'm here," Jacob said. "When you find him, maybe … you should spare him."

"Are you mad?" the general asked.

"Trust me, I want to strangle that coward myself. But this isn't about what I want, or what you want, or what makes us feel better for not protecting Whistler. I think if we go around firing bullets, we'll only make things worse. That's not what Whistler wants."

Rommond sighed. Brooklyn clenched his hand a little tighter and gave him a reassuring nod.

"I suppose you're right," the general said. "Vengeance doesn't heal wounds, does it?"

"It makes new ones," Brooklyn said.

"Never got to say it before, but good to see you back," Jacob said, saluting Brooklyn. "Did you complete your mission?"

"I did, and that is why I'm here."

Rommond straightened up. "Oh?"

"I made journey of discovery. The spirits are not just in machines. They are in nature, in everything, even in Glass." He took a small crystal shard from his pocket, which glimmered as if it were responding to him. "I hear not just one language, but many dialects. For long the spirits of machine were at war with spirits of nature, but they seek peace, like we seek peace, and they can achieve that peace … through us."

"A year ago I would have doubted you," Rommond said, "but then a year ago I thought you were dead. Let life surprise me then, for some of them have been pleasant."

"I now understand Glass like I understand iron," Brooklyn continued. "I see in its deep veins same anatomy I see in wires and cables. All things live. To bring them together, it is not so much matter of engineering as it is matter of diplomacy. True engineers are just ambassadors for lives of all things."

Rommond looked very eager, and seemed to be fighting his desire to urge Brooklyn to get to the point. Jacob could tell he was building up to something, that he was almost working it out right then and there before them.

The tribesman produced a large schematic, with many fine details. It showed a kind of mobile missile launcher, with giant rotating treads, and what looked like crystal missiles. There were so many tiny parts of the drawing, with many explanatory notes in the tribesman's language, and what looked like symbols from languages that no one else there present knew, that the sight was immediately overwhelming.

While Jacob's face was bewildered, Rommond's was pasted with an open smile. "Brooklyn's back," he said.

"What is it?" Jacob asked.

Brooklyn gestured to the drawing. "This is landship without weapons."

"Then what are these?" Jacob pointed to the missile-like objects.

"Concentrated Glass. It tears a hole in space,

through which we may move."

"A Rift," the general said. "Like the one the demons came through."

"The *marans* came through," Jacob corrected. "So … what good is this?"

"We take back our home by taking theirs," Rommond said.

"But isn't it barren?"

"It is empty of many things," Brooklyn explained, "but spirits live there too, and know it has great secret—why people from there do not get well."

"The Iron Plague?"

"They are controlled by him, and by their fear of disease, and lust for cure. When they see that he keeps them that way, they will not follow. They will break their chains like I broke my ones made of wire."

"This could end the war," Rommond said.

"It will end," Brooklyn stated, "one way or other way."

"I almost dare not ask," Jacob said, pointing to the schematic of the missile launcher, "but does it have a name?"

"No," Brooklyn said. "I am not good with names." He turned to Rommond.

"I've got one," the general said, and his smile was now infectious. "The Hometaker."

About the Author

Dean F. Wilson was born in Dublin, Ireland in 1987. He started writing at age 11, when he began his first (unpublished) novel, entitled *The Power Source*. He won a TAP Educational Award from Trinity College Dublin for an early draft of *The Call of Agon* (then called *Protos Mythos*) in 2001.

He is the author of the *Children of Telm* epic fantasy trilogy and the *Great Iron War* steampunk series.

Dean also works as a journalist, primarily in the field of technology. He has written for *TechEye*, *Thinq*, *V3*, *VR-Zone*, *ITProPortal*, *TechRadar Pro*, and *The Inquirer*.

www.deanfwilson.com